Courteous, courageous and commanding—
these heroes lay it all on the line for the
people they love in more than fifty stories about
loyalty, bravery and romance.
Don't miss a single one!

AVAILABLE MAY 2010
Special Assignment: Baby by Debra Webb
My Baby, My Love by Dani Sinclair
The Sheriff's Proposal by Karen Rose Smith
The Marriage Conspiracy by Christine Rimmer
The Woman for Dusty Conrad by Tori Carrington
The White Night by Stella Bagwell
Code Name: Prince by Valerie Parv

AVAILABLE JUNE 2010
Same Place, Same Time by C.J. Carmichael
One Last Chance by Justine Davis
By Leaps and Bounds by Jacqueline Diamond
Too Many Brothers by Roz Denny Fox
Secretly Married by Allison Leigh
Strangers When We Meet by Rebecca Winters

AVAILABLE JULY 2010
Babe in the Woods by Caroline Burnes
Serving Up Trouble by Jill Shalvis
Deputy Daddy by Carla Cassidy
The Major and the Librarian by Nikki Benjamin
A Family Man by Mindy Neff
The President's Daughter by Annette Broadrick
Return to Tomorrow by Marisa Carroll

AVAILABLE AUGUST 2010
Remember My Touch by Gayle Wilson
Return of the Lawman by Lisa Childs
If You Don't Know by Now by Teresa Southwick
Surprise Inheritance by Charlotte Douglas
Snowbound Bride by Cathy Gillen Thacker
The Good Daughter by Jean Brashear

AVAILABLE SEPTEMBER 2010
The Hero's Son by Amanda Stevens
Secret Witness by Jessica Andersen
On Pins and Needles by Victoria Pade
Daddy in Dress Blues by Cathie Linz
AKA: Marriage by Jule McBride
Pregnant and Protected by Lilian Darcy

USA TODAY Bestselling Author

MARIE FERRARELLA

FIVE-ALARM AFFAIR

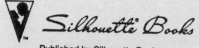

Published by Silhouette Books
America's Publisher of Contemporary Romance

SILHOUETTE BOOKS
®

ISBN-13: 978-0-373-36253-0

FIVE-ALARM AFFAIR

Copyright © 1988 by Marie Rydzynski-Ferrarella

PLEASE RECYCLE
THIS PRODUCT IS RECYCLABLE

Recycling programs
for this product may
not exist in your area.

This edition published by arrangement with Harlequin Books S.A.

For questions and comments about the quality of this book please contact us at Customer_eCare@Harlequin.ca.

Visit Silhouette Books at www.eHarlequin.com

Printed in U.S.A.

MARIE FERRARELLA

This *USA TODAY* bestselling and RITA® Award-winning author has written almost two hundred novels for Silhouette Books, some under the name Marie Nicole. Her romances are beloved by fans worldwide. Visit her Web site at www.marieferrarella.com.

To Helen Conrad,
God's most precious creation,
A perfect best friend.

Chapter 1

The scream brought her to her feet with a jolt. The cup by her hand, half-filled with lukewarm coffee, tipped over. Its contents puddled on her oak desk, stopping just short of the papers she'd been working so hard on. One moment Aimee Greer was juggling writing a report on the latest swim meet scores with writing up the highlights of a two-story fixer-upper that *had* no highlights. The next moment she was dashing out of her second-floor den, her heart pounding.

Heather!

Heather was screaming. Heather never screamed. Aimee's ten-year-old daughter had a thing about being nonchalant. What could have caused her stoic tomboy to scream? A myriad of disasters flashed through Aimee's brain as she dashed down the stairs. Her answer came wrapped in sheets of smoke—smoke that was wafting out of the kitchen into the dining room as she got to the bottom of the stairs.

Fire! Stay calm, Aimee. Panic later.

"Heather!" Aimee dashed into the kitchen. "Are you all right? Where are you?"

"Here."

Heather's voice was full of fear. With good reason. She had drawn back as far as she could in the kitchen and was staring at the fire on the stove. Flames were fanning out of a frying pan, threatening to link long yellow-red fingers with the rest of the house.

Aimee immediately shut off the stove, then jumped back, out of range of the heat.

Fire extinguisher. Damn it, where had she put that thing? She had bought it because it was the right thing to do and had meant to hang it up as soon as she'd walked into the house with it. That had been three weeks ago.

Think, Aimee, before your kitchen becomes history.

The cabinet next to the stove!

Aimee made a wide circle around the stove and its flaming pan, watching it warily like the unpredictable enemy it was. Tottering on her bare toes, Aimee tried to get into the overhead cabinet. She glanced at her daughter.

Heather watched her, hardly daring to breathe, transformed from an independent soul into a frightened child. "Mother?" she quavered.

"It's going to be fine, Heather." Aimee thought she sounded a hell of a lot calmer than she felt. "Your dad always claimed I had asbestos fingers." She succeeded in opening the cabinet door, grabbed the canister and yanked it out. Several glasses tumbled out in the process and shattered on the tile countertop. Heather gasped, then covered her mouth with her hands.

Now what? Aimee had never used an extinguisher before, and it felt foreign and clumsy in her hands.

This was no time to stop and read directions. She ripped the top off the canister and pressed the only thing she could find to depress. The unexpected force of the chemical foam that poured out almost made her drop the canister. Drawing a deep breath, Aimee got a better grip on the canister and aimed the nozzle at the body of the fire.

"You're getting it!" Heather squealed, some of her normal buoyancy returning.

"Of course I'm getting it. I'm your mother."

One. Two. Three. Seconds or minutes? Aimee wasn't quite certain. Finally, the fire died out, and nothing was left but a blackened pan that held two indistinguishable lumps. The air was heavy with the smell of smoke, despite the open window. The wallpaper on either side of the stove was no longer yellow. It was dark, as were the curtains that hung by the window on the other side of the stove.

Aimee swallowed, and her heart moved back down from her throat and into her chest. She sagged against the sink counter. The spent canister hung suspended from her numbed fingertips.

"Heather, what was all that about?" To her own ears

she sounded as if she were asking about the plot of a television program, not why Heather had almost managed to burn down their house. But Aimee knew there was no point in making an accusation; Heather had been frightened enough.

Heather dropped her gaze and looked at the floor. "I wanted to surprise you."

Aimee drew a long breath. "A fire in the kitchen would be one way to do it, yes." She raised her arm, and Heather slipped in under the protective arch, seeming relieved that there was no lecture forthcoming. Aimee said gently, "Couldn't you have surprised me with something a little less dramatic?"

"I was trying to make dinner."

"The fire belongs under the pan, honey, not in it."

Heather shrugged her thin shoulders, and her baggy blue school sweatshirt moved askew. "I guess I had the temperature too high."

Aimee laughed as relief took over. "Way too high." She deposited the empty extinguisher in the garbage pail beneath the sink, then looked around at the wallpaper. It had taken her so long to hang it just right, and now half of it was ruined. She foresaw more long hours with paste and uncooperative rolls of wallpaper and tried not to think about it.

"C'mon, help me find my shoes. It's fast food tonight for us, kid."

Heather looked around guiltily. "Don't you want to clean up?"

"Clean up is the *last* thing I want to do now. As Scarlett O'Hara said—" Aimee dramatically placed a hand on her forehead "'—I'll think about that tomorrow.'" She ran her finger down Heather's short nose. "Maybe it won't look so bad in the light of day." But I doubt it, she added silently.

"I think you left your shoes upstairs in your office," Heather offered.

"Would you please get them for me, honey?" Heather bounded out of the room, and Aimee called after her, "And don't surprise me with anything for a while. Deal?"

"Deal!"

Aimee thought about the work upstairs that she still had to do and tried to figure out how she would fit into her schedule this latest development—an unexpected redecorating job. Her time was budgeted practically down to the quarter hour as it was.

A wailing noise cut into Aimee's thoughts just as Heather reached the bottom of the stairs, holding Aimee's shoes. Fire engines.

"You don't think…?" Aimee couldn't bring herself to finish the sentence.

Heather dashed to the front window in the living room. "They're stopping here," she confirmed excitedly.

"Terrific." Aimee sighed. "It must have been Mr. Peabody," she muttered, feeling suddenly weary.

Their kitchen faced his house. Mr. Peabody worried about inflation, taxes, stray dogs and helpless women who lived alone—and so had appointed himself

Aimee's guardian in absentia. Aimee had philosophically decided that everyone needed a hobby, and she was Mr. Peabody's.

The doorbell rang. Thank goodness they don't chop their way in like they do in the cartoons, Aimee thought. She ran her hand through her curly blond hair, trying to bring order to the mass. She threw the door open, wearing her biggest apologetic smile, expecting to see Matt Baron, chief of the local fire station. As she looked up at the man in the doorway, her breath caught.

He was a stranger—a very big, handsome stranger—and Aimee didn't tend to see a lot of strangers. Greenfield, California, wasn't a large city, and Aimee, as a real estate agent, PTA member, swim meet coordinator, Little League supporter and library fundraiser, had come to know a great many people in it, at least by sight…and the man before her, who had wall-to-wall shoulders, wide green eyes and, under his helmet, what looked like dark blond hair, was certainly a sight.

A familiar voice came from behind the tall stranger. "Aimee?" She was brought back to her senses, feeling a little foolish.

"Matt! Matt, I'm so sorry," she said, though her eyes never left the tall, blond fireman, who regarded her with mild curiosity.

The thought occurred to her that if he wasn't married, half of Greenfield's unattached women would soon be laying siege to his door.

She blinked and cleared her throat, stepping back to

let them through the door. Again she ran her hand through her wayward hair.

She was married, Wayne thought, seeing the wedding ring on her finger, and couldn't understand why such a wave of disappointment came over him. He'd known her for all of five seconds. He'd felt physical attraction before, but never quite this hard.

Matt had pushed his way in past the blond fireman and was now looking oddly at Aimee. She was sure he'd noted the fleeting stunned expression on her face. Matt had known Aimee ever since she'd been in junior high, where his younger sister had been in her class. Aimee watched as he scanned the house. "So what happened? Where's the fire, Aimee?"

Suddenly she needed the comforting presence of an old friend. There was something that totally unnerved her about her reaction to the unknown fireman. "The fire was in a frying pan." She pointed behind her, toward the kitchen, which was still adrift in a smokey cloud.

"Dinner," Heather interjected ruefully.

"She tried to surprise me," Aimee added with a grin. She slipped her arm around Heather in a gesture of support—not that, she thought, Heather needed it. Heather had been independent since birth. Or pretended to be.

Matt shook his head reprovingly. "Why can't your kid be like mine and try to get *out* of doing chores?" Heather stood for it good-naturedly. Matt waved one of the firemen into the kitchen to make sure that the threat was over.

Aimee looked toward the stranger, who towered over

Matt. There was a rugged quality to his face, rugged yet kindly. His nose looked as if it had once been on the receiving end of a punch. Not crooked, just not perfect. Character, she mused. And something more. But she wouldn't have reacted so dramatically to him if her mind hadn't been going in three directions at once.

She gave him a disparaging smile.

"Everything's okay, chief," the third fireman reported back to Matt, who barely nodded in acknowledgment.

Aimee suddenly became aware of the fact that Heather was still holding her shoes. She took them and began to slip into them, putting one hand on Matt's shoulder to steady herself. To her surprise, the blond fireman knelt down to help her. His cool fingers along the side of her foot created an unaccustomed warmth within her.

"I didn't know you were a frustrated shoe salesman, Montgomery," Matt quipped.

"Just like helping a lady in distress," the stranger, Montgomery, said. His gaze held hers as he helped her on with the other shoe. She felt as if it were all happening in slow motion.

She searched for something to say. "Heather, throw the rest of the windows open, please."

Montgomery rose, and Aimee suddenly felt as if she needed air. "Thank you."

"Anytime," he replied warmly.

She didn't answer. Instead, she looked at Matt. "Can I make amends by offering you and your crew something to drink?"

Matt removed his helmet and shook his head, muttering, "Damn thing makes my head sweat." To Aimee he replied, "I guess we'll just think of it as a practice run. Any idea who might have called this in?"

"Probably Mr. Peabody."

As she spoke, a compact man of anywhere from sixty to seventy—he wasn't about to tell—bustled his way in.

"Aimee, are you all right?" he demanded in his fussy voice.

His words were tinged with a New England accent, Wayne thought, and he wondered how many people concerned themselves with this woman's life.

"Just fine, Mr. Peabody," she answered cheerfully. "No cause for alarm."

"No cause? When there's smoke belching out of your kitchen window?"

"Just crepes with too much heat under them," she answered lightly.

Peabody shook his head. "You'd think a woman your age would know how to cook."

"You'd think that, wouldn't you?" Aimee answered cheerfully.

Wayne watched Aimee as she moved through the room and back to the kitchen. He was aware that Matt and the other firemen were edging their way to the door, but something about the petite blonde woman held his attention even when he knew that he should be leaving with them.

He was new to the area and hadn't yet quite found

his place. Growing up in Los Angeles hadn't exactly prepared him for the closeness of a budding new city. But this was what he had been looking for, something friendlier and stabler than was available in a big city. He liked the easy pace in Greenfield, but he was finding it difficult to lose the stigma of being an outsider. Other than the two times Matt had had him over to dinner and Matt's wife had tried to fix him up with a different woman each time, Wayne hadn't really had a date in the five weeks since he'd left L.A.

Had this woman been single, he mused, he would have changed his dateless status.

Matt interrupted his reverie, calling, "Montgomery, you coming, or are you going to play Smokey the Bear and guard the frying pan to see if it plans to reignite?"

Aimee looked over her shoulder and directed her words at Matt, but her eyes were on the new man in town. "Thanks for stopping by. I'll rest easier knowing that the fire department is so prompt."

"I'll rest easier if you give the kid some cooking lessons," Matt muttered as he closed the door behind them.

As they got back aboard the fire truck, Wayne asked, "How long has she been married?"

"She's not."

Wayne felt a strange sort of lightening of his spirit at Matt's words.

"She's a widow."

"Oh? Who is she? What's her name?"

Matt gave the signal, and the driver started up the rig. "Aimee Greer. Interested?"

"You might say that." Wayne hung on as the driver took a corner.

"Damn kid needs to go back to driver's ed," Matt grumbled. He glanced at Wayne. "Don't be."

After having gone along good-naturedly with Matt's wife's matchmaking ventures, Wayne was surprised at his superior's warning. "Why? Is she taken?"

"Yes."

"But you just said she wasn't married."

"That's right. She's not."

Wayne gripped the side of the truck as another corner whipped by. "Engaged?"

"No."

"Possessed," Wayne quipped, running out of options.

Matt grinned, then grew serious. "Aimee grew up around here. She and her husband, Terry, left when they got married. Terry was killed in a car accident, oh, I guess six years ago. She came back here with her daughter to live."

Six years was a long time for a woman to be alone, Wayne mused. Especially one who looked like Aimee. He found himself becoming more and more intrigued. "There haven't been any men?"

"Have there been men!" Matt laughed, then sobered slightly when he saw Wayne's speculative look. "No, not that way. Oh, they were interested in her, all right. Guys have always been interested in Aimee. But she doesn't want anyone, not that way. She's made that point loud and clear. She's just not interested. She has a habit of turning the most passionate-minded suitors into friends." Matt grinned broadly. "Aimee has lots and lots of friends. She's driven my wife and sister crazy."

"Why?"

"They want to see her married. You know how women are," he said genially.

"Not really. I had two older brothers, and my mother died when I was three. I haven't all that much experience with 'how women are.'" But suddenly, he thought, he wanted to change that.

"Take my advice and don't start your education with Aimee—not unless you want to know what it feels like to be put out to pasture."

For the first time since he had moved to Greenfield, Wayne felt the thrill of a challenge. "You're intriguing me."

Matt shook his head. "I was afraid of that."

The firehouse, a small, modern building that was buffered on both sides by large empty fields, came into view. Wayne asked, "Is Phyllis up to another dinner?"

"Phyllis is *always* up to another dinner. She considers you one of her failures."

"Failure?" Wayne laughed. "She's only tried twice."

"To a born matchmaker, that should be enough to do the trick."

"How about having me over to dinner and inviting Aimee?"

Matt shrugged. "Your funeral."

Wayne jumped off the truck before it came to a halt. He thought of Aimee's full, upturned mouth and the inviting curves he had noted beneath the jeans and striped T-shirt. More than that, he thought of the humor he had seen in her eyes. Definitely a woman who looked like she was worth getting to know. Wayne was in the market for something more than just a no-strings relationship, and something told him Aimee Greer was just what he was looking for. At least it was worth exploring. "Maybe it'll be my funeral, but somehow I don't think so."

"That's what they all say," Matt replied forebodingly.

Wayne was willing to take his chances.

Chapter 2

Aimee closed the door after the firemen had left. She closed her eyes and pressed her back against the door. Thank heavens that was over.

She turned around, and for a moment she was startled. She was facing the accusing eyes of Emmett J. Peabody. Somehow she'd thought he'd left with the others. Avoiding his eyes, she allowed herself a small sigh as she crossed the entranceway and walked back into the kitchen, her nose wrinkling at the smell of smoke.

She surveyed the damage. No two ways about it. She was going to have to pull off that wallpaper. She hated wallpapering, too. Maybe if she and Heather scraped it off and just painted instead…

Emmett had followed her into the kitchen. He said nothing, but she could feel his eyes assessing her. Aimee waited impatiently for him to begin his lecture. The sooner he did, the sooner she could usher him to the door.

"All right, Emmett, out with it." She didn't bother to turn around. "What's on your mind?" She picked up one of the limp curtains that framed the window. The metal rod, weakened by the intense heat, sagged in the middle, then broke. It clattered into the sink.

Giving her mother a weak smile, Heather picked up the remains of the curtain and rod and shoved them into the garbage.

"You almost burned down the block. What should be on my mind?"

Aimee laughed as she turned around. Her gaze swept over the man in the neatly pressed slacks and partially buttoned cardigan. He'd become family to her when she'd needed a family most, so she frequently forgave him his transgressions.

"We—I," she corrected herself, nodding at Heather, "didn't even burn down the room, much less the block, Emmett." She coaxed him good-naturedly, "C'mon, I can tell a lecture's coming on. Might as well get it over with."

Clearing his throat, he sank his hands defiantly into the pockets of his cardigan and pugnaciously raised his somewhat receding chin. "I don't lecture, Aimee. I merely observe and comment."

She crossed her arms. "And just what is it you *observed?*"

"That if you were married, this wouldn't have happened."

Whatever she'd been expecting, Aimee thought, it wasn't this. This was a topic he pulled out during Sunday brunches or when they sat out on the patio and talked after she returned from an evening appointment with a client.

"Oh, come *on,* Emmett. That's absolutely ridiculous. What possible difference would my being married have made in this situation?" She waited to see what he'd come up with this time; he could be very creative.

"He'd be supporting you so that you wouldn't have to be doing a thousand and one things. Then you'd have time to concentrate on cooking, instead of leaving it to burn." His voice softened. "Aimee, a girl like you shouldn't live by herself."

"I'm not living by myself, Emmett." She put her arm around Heather's shoulders. The girl fit in just under her arm, coming up to her chest. "I have Heather."

She smiled at her daughter warmly. Having Heather to be responsible for had seen her through that very rough period of her life six years ago. Having Heather meant the world to her. She looked back at Emmett. "And I'm hardly a girl."

He peered at her over the tops of his half glasses. "Missy, to me any female under the age of sixty is a girl." He permitted a misty smile to crease his thin lips. "My Martha was a girl until the day she died."

Aimee regarded Emmett with no small amount of affection. "Haven't you heard about women's lib? We're all *women* now."

Heather nodded smartly, concurring with her mother's statement.

Emmett gave them both a pained look and waved his hand dismissively at Aimee. "Shows what they know. The two are mixed. A sixty-year-old lady can laugh and you know in your heart that there's a young girl still in there, still playful, with a girl's light heart."

He was talking about his late wife. They had been married forty-one years when she died, Aimee recalled. It had been her turn to offer Emmett comfort then. Shortly after that, Emmett's daughter, Cynthia, and her husband, Ray, had moved in with him. Emmett had pretended to grumble about the inconvenience, but Aimee knew he was delighted not to have to live alone in the house.

"I'll concede that point," Aimee granted.

He nodded knowingly. "I had a feeling you might."

She didn't want him to get on a roll. He was a darling man, but he had a habit of going on and on if given half a chance. And at the moment, all she wanted was to get something into her rumbling stomach and return to her work.

"But not your other point. I'm perfectly happy living just the way I am. Times have changed, Emmett." She patted his cheek, and he made a show of pulling back. "A woman doesn't need a man around to be complete."

A gray brow arched, and he leveled his gaze at her. "Doesn't she?"

She let out a sharp breath. "Mr. Peabody." There was a warning in her voice.

"Now she gets formal," he quipped in an aside to Heather.

She would try just one more time, Aimee thought. After all, he did a lot for her, and he was her surrogate father, so to speak, what with her own parents in Florida for the past ten years. "Emmett, I've been blessed with a very happy marriage. I don't want a replacement. My memories will last me for the rest of my life."

He made a disgruntled noise. "You're too young to live in the past."

"And you're too young to spend the evening badgering me. Isn't there some nice senior lady you'd like to see or—" She broke off, looking at him hopefully.

Despite his cranky mien, Emmett Peabody was the most social creature she knew of, barring Margo. He belonged to countless senior citizens' groups and held the felicitous position of being one of the few eligible men around among scores of widows.

"Not tonight," he replied. "Thought I'd take a break and stay home." He looked around the kitchen as if seeing it for the first time. He shook his head, clucking sympathetically. "I'd say you've got your work cut out for you."

Aimee sighed. "I can probably fit it in between 10:32 and 11:02 on Sunday."

She caught Heather's guilty look and gave her hand an affectionate squeeze. It wasn't really Heather's fault. Heather was trying. Maybe in his own way Emmett was right. Maybe she should cut back. But where? She needed to be on top of all those properties she listed under her name. And then there were those committees she was on, most of which involved Heather. And then there was—

Emmett commented, "You've got enough projects for any three women."

She flushed. "Well, I—"

"If you had a man around the house—" he began loftily.

Time to head him off at the pass, she decided. "Then I'd have enough projects for any four women."

He pursed his lips, withdrawing for the time being. "Need any help with that?" He waved a hand at the kitchen wall.

She led him toward the front door, picking up her purse from the family room sofa as she made her way. "I'll manage."

He stopped just short of the door. "You always do, somehow, Aimee. Cynthia's husband gets stationed overseas and she has trouble figuring out how many stamps to put on the envelope." He shook his head at his daughter's incompetence.

"That's because you used to make all her decisions for her. You never let her think for herself," Aimee pointed out.

"Yeah, well, maybe."

Aimee opened the door, and he began to walk out, saying, "Oh, I almost forgot. Cynthia wants to know if you'll be needing her tonight to stay with Heather."

Aimee shook her head. "A colleague is taking all my

calls tonight. I was supposed to stay home and do some work, before my…impromptu barbecue." She threaded her fingers through Heather's. "Now we'll go off for some burgers, right, Heather?"

"Actually, it all turned out pretty neat, huh?" Heather said enthusiastically. She loved fast food.

Aimee gave her a reproving look.

"Well, maybe not so neat," Heather amended, staring down at her tennis shoes.

Emmett looked over at his own house. "I suppose I'd better be going home."

"You're welcome to come with us," Aimee offered, locking the door behind them.

He gave her a startled look. "Do you know what they *put* in those hamburgers?"

"No, and I don't want to know. Sometimes ignorance is bliss," she informed him cheerfully, then looked down at Heather. "Okay, let's go, kid."

It was after midnight when Aimee finally gave up the battle with her paperwork and crawled into bed. Heather had long since disappeared into her room.

Aimee opened one of the two windows bracketing her bed, and a gentle breeze floated in. The suburban block was quiet. Only the crickets calling to one another broke the silence, blending with the faint throb of music that came through the wall between Aimee's and Heather's bedrooms. Aimee couldn't understand how, but the noise soothed Heather to sleep.

Aimee rolled over on her back, wide-awake. After all the excitement and then all the work, she'd have thought she wouldn't even have been able to make it to bed before she fell asleep. After all, she'd fallen asleep many times at her desk, her head cradled in her arms, surrounded by descriptions of new listings. Tonight, however, she felt oddly restless, as if something nagged at her.

The moon was full and bright and shone in through her window, illuminating the wood-framed portrait that hung on the wall opposite her bed. Her wedding portrait.

They looked so young in that picture, she thought now. She and Terry had still been in school, still full of life's promise. It seemed that she had known him forever; she'd set her cap for him between fifth and sixth grade. It had taken him a few years to come around, she thought with a smile, but he had. At fifteen he gave her his school ring. For her eighteenth birthday, an engagement ring. They were married a little more than a year later. In her heart, she'd been married to him all her life, since he'd been part of every thought, every memory, for so long.

She closed her eyes as she felt the tears welling up. After all these years, the pain was still fresh. His death had come so unexpectedly. He had been driving home from work and someone had jumped the center divider on the road and ended all their dreams in one fateful act.

She had died when the police had come to notify her. She'd cried for twenty-four hours straight, and then she'd submerged her hurt in a thousand details that kept her busy. No one around her would ever have guessed that at the center of her was a core of pain that made her vow never to be left so bereft again.

For two weeks after his death, while she'd maintained a brave front for Terry's friends and relatives, she'd felt like an empty shell. She'd gone through the motions, wondering why life had gone on after Terry's death. Then she'd pulled herself together, squaring her shoulders and her soul and sailing off into life full steam ahead.

With one exception.

She didn't let her heart out of bondage. All her friends, most especially Matt's wife, Phyllis, were forever trying to fix her up with every bachelor they came across. They'd invite her to dinner, and there, sitting across from her, would be a man who just happened to be unattached and just happened to have dropped in. Aimee stood for it all with humor and patience, knowing that her friends' matchmaking attempts were out of concern and love. But she never permitted anything to materialize from any of these arranged encounters except friendship.

She sighed, moving around restlessly under the covers. The last thing she saw when she closed her eyes was her wedding picture. But the image in her mind's eye was not that of her dark-haired, aristocratic-featured husband. The face she conjured up was broad, with an easy smile, green eyes and dark blond hair.

Aimee's eyes flew open in surprise and the image vanished.

Red Foley, the office comedian, had made up an anniversary card with a picture of the Maxwell mansion on the cover. It was meant to be a tongue-in-cheek celebration of the mansion's ninth month with the agency. He dropped off a card on each agent's desk before the office manager arrived. The Maxwell mansion, built sixty years earlier, before the city of Greenfield had enjoyed its healthy growth spurt, was the agency's white elephant.

Although she had a soft spot in her heart for the fixer-upper mansion, Aimee regarded her card without a smile, her mind elsewhere.

"You look a little worn-out today, kiddo. Wanna talk about it?" Margo Fontaine peered at Aimee over her huge coffee mug.

Aimee looked at the woman whose desk was juxtaposed to hers in the Rialto Realty office. Margo, a three-time grandmother, worked at the real estate office part-time because she liked to talk to people, not because she needed a source of income. Her approach to sales was lax. If she sold a house, so much the better, but she wasn't about to kill herself to do it. Her main function was to talk, to share life with people instead of with a television set.

The short, round-faced woman with the halo of
fluffy beige hair had made herself Aimee's chief con-
fidante. Not that Aimee had much to confide, she had
once observed to Aimee. Aimee was open, and everyone got the same information out of her. There were no
secrets, as far as Aimee was concerned. Still, Margo
kept on trying. "Ahem. I said, 'Do you want to talk
about it?'"

"I didn't get much sleep last night," Aimee explained.

Margo leaned forward, propping up her ample arms
on her desk. She even stopped munching on her huge
sweet roll, which rested now on top of Foley's card.

"This sounds interesting." Her eyes sparkled with
anticipation. "What's his name?"

Aimee suddenly had a clear image of the blond
fireman and realized at that moment that *he* had been responsible for her sleeplessness. She looked at Margo,
banishing his face from her mind. That was all she needed
to do—tell Margo that some fireman whose first name she
didn't even know had kept her awake. The older woman
would quite gleefully jump to a very wrong conclusion,
envisioning the pair engaged in a torrid night of passion.

"It wasn't a him, Margo," Aimee told her. She began
to search through her desk for her book of listings. "It
was an it."

Margo's smile grew broader. "That sounds kinky. I
need details."

Aimee looked at her. "Margo, you're something else."

Margo popped another piece of the sweet roll into her mouth. "That's what Edgar keeps mumbling." She shook her head disparagingly. "The man won't read any of those self-help books I keep giving him."

Aimee smothered a grin. "Sex manuals, Margo. You mean sex manuals." Where *was* that listings book of hers? She looked around the office. Bob must have borrowed it. He was always losing his.

"Whatever."

Aimee had met Edgar Fontaine on two separate occasions. He was a tired, mousy little man who could not begin to live up to his wife's expectations. Aimee felt a little sorry for both of them. "I think you're being too hard on poor Edgar."

"A person is never too old to learn. Now then—" she gave Aimee the full benefit of her attention "—we're not talking about my love life or lack thereof. We're talking about yours."

"Or lack thereof," Aimee finished for her. She called to a man who just entered the office, "Bob, do you have my book of listings?" A sheepish grin was her answer. Aimee put out her hands. "Give it here." She turned toward Margo to answer her question. "I had a fire at the house."

Margo drew her lips together in concern. "Is Heather okay?"

"Everything's fine except for the wallpaper." Aimee accepted the worn leather-bound book from Bob, who mumbled an apology before he loped off to his desk.

"Heather tried to surprise me with dinner and got a little carried away. Mr. Peabody called the fire department."

Margo blew out a breath. "That old man would. No wonder you look so harried."

Aimee gave serious thought to making a quick trip to the ladies' room to check her face. "Margo, your flattery'll turn my head."

Margo's eyes grew large. "Speak of turning heads, who's *that?*"

Aimee's desk faced the far wall in the office, and she could not see the conference room door. Margo could. And from the expression on her face, whatever she saw now made her mouth drop open.

"Margo, it isn't seemly for a fifty-eight—"

"Fifty-two," Margo corrected her, never looking away from the doorway.

"—year-old grandmother to drool. You're getting Foley's card all wet." Aimee laughed, easing her swivel chair around to see who had caught the woman's lascivious eye.

"I didn't know there were rules on when and when not to drool," Margo retorted, then said under her breath, "And if there was, he'd be the exception no matter what the rule."

"Margo, I—" Aimee's words died in her throat. It took her a moment to place him. His blond hair was a little unruly, as if he had forgotten to run a comb through it after the wind had gotten to it. He wore jeans, a jersey and a windbreaker, and without his uniform he looked different, less serious.

And a lot more threatening, she thought suddenly.

Now, why had she thought that? she wondered, startled.

"Yes?" Margo looked at her suddenly silent partner, then back at the stranger, who was walking in their direction. "Does take your breath away, doesn't he? Aimee, he's heading in this direction. Sit up straight."

"You sound like my mother," Aimee quipped. Maybe she should have popped into the bathroom to check out her appearance…. What was she *thinking?* What difference could her appearance possibly make to either of them? Unconsciously, she smoothed down the skirt of her cream linen suit.

He stopped before Aimee's desk and placed one hand on the back of her chair. She thought the gesture oddly possessive, then told herself she was suffering from a lack of sleep. And possible smoke inhalation.

Something seemed to melt inside of her when he looked down into her face and smiled. "Hi."

"Hi." The word took considerable effort to push out. What *was* the matter with her? "Did Matt send you out to check if I turned off the stove before I left the house?" she asked lightly.

Wayne found he wanted to trace her smile with his lips. She was having an incredible effect on him, he marveled. "As a matter of fact…"

"You're kidding." She looked at him in surprise. "Matt's getting a little overprotective."

"This is a fireman?" Margo interjected.

Aimee suddenly remembered where she was. "Um, Margo Fontaine, this is…" She stopped. "I don't know your first name, Mr. Montgomery." *Don't tell me your name. I don't want to know anything about you,* she thought, a sudden stab of panic flashing through her.

"It's Wayne. Wayne Montgomery." He nodded politely at Margo, then looked back at Aimee. "And no, Matt isn't being overprotective. He's being a host."

Aimee blinked. "Excuse me?"

Wayne hoped he could keep a straight face as he recited the invitation. "He sent me over to ask you to come to his house tomorrow night for a dinner party."

"I've always loved the personal touch," Margo interjected, sighing. "I never rated anything more than a phone call from any of my hosts."

Aimee smelled a rat. A rat who wore a fire chief's hat. "This is rather sudden, isn't it?" she said wryly.

"Rather," Wayne agreed. And what would she say if he told her he'd talked Matt into it? he wondered.

"Are you going to be there?" She kept her suspicion out of her face but not her eyes.

"Yes."

"Bingo!" Margo cried.

Aimee gave her a sharp look that made her retreat into temporary silence. "I see," Aimee murmured.

Yes, he imagined she did. She was bright. He liked

that. When he went out with a woman, he wanted someone who was his equal on all levels.

Aimee hadn't been far from his thoughts since he'd first seen her yesterday. He'd used the excuse of personally delivering Matt's invitation in order to see her again. He'd hoped that his reaction to her would be different in the light of day.

It wasn't. And it wasn't because of anything that he could knowingly define, like her physical assets. No, there was something more to it than that. Something in her eyes. Something that called to him.

"Matt suggested that I pick you up tomorrow night."

"Oh, he did, did he?" she asked sweetly.

Wayne saw the look that passed over her face and wondered if she was plotting Matt's demise. He wouldn't put it past her. He found himself liking her more and more. "Will seven be all right?"

"Seven will be fine." Aimee mused that she'd have Matt drawn and quartered first, then grilled on a rack—or maybe the other way around.

"Well, I'd better let you get back to your work," Wayne said, and left, content with laying the groundwork for the next move.

"*That* was your fireman?" Margo said after Wayne took his leave.

"He was one of them." Aimee tried to sound casual. His unexpected visit had thrown her more than she wanted to admit.

Margo stared dreamily at the closed door. "How did you notice anyone else when he was in the room?"

Aimee began to thumb through her listings book but realized that she'd forgotten what she was looking for. "Down, Margo. Remember your blood pressure."

"*You* remember it. I'm having too much fun fantasizing." She reached out over her desk and squeezed Aimee's arm. "And you get to go out with him."

Only for dinner at Matt's house—if she let Matt live that long, she mused. "You make him sound like the Irish Sweepstakes."

"Hell, no. The Irish Sweepstakes is only money. This is a lot better."

Was it? Aimee thought as she turned back to the notes on her desk. There was something about Mr. Wayne Montgomery, a premonition perhaps, that made her nervous. She wondered if she was doing the right thing in agreeing to go to this dinner party. Then she told herself she was being silly.

Chapter 3

Aimee looked at her watch. Ten o'clock. A client was coming to the office at ten-thirty—which gave Aimee precisely half an hour to have a talk with her self-appointed Cupid in rubber boots. He had to stop this sort of thing.

Aimee dialed the firehouse number. Someone picked up and said, "Oak Street Firehouse."

Aimee couldn't mistake Matt's deep, gravelly voice. She reminded herself that Matt was an old friend who was motivated by concern. "I'd like a word with you, Matt."

"Oh, hi, Aimee."

She detected a forced nonchalance in his voice. She picked up a pencil and began doodling.

"Cooking up anything special in your kitchen tonight?" he asked.

She sketched a very elaborate noose. "Very funny, Matt. I'm not calling to talk to you about last night."

"Er...yeah, well." He cleared his throat. "I'm rather busy here right now."

"Matt." The single word said it all: *hang up and you're dead.*

She heard a resigned sigh. "Yeah?"

Aimee's doodling was beginning to take on major proportions. "Why is Phyllis suddenly having a dinner party?"

"Aw, you know Phyl, Aimee. She likes to bring people together."

Aimee began to draw in the scaffold. "She also likes plenty of time to plan everything. Like two to three weeks. This is just one day, Matt. That's awfully short notice for her."

"She's turned over a new leaf."

A figure wearing a fireman's hat was beginning to take form. She drew him in on the scaffold beneath the noose. "I have a feeling you're behind all this."

"Aimee, Aimee, Aimee," Matt said with a sigh. "Just give the guy a chance."

With that last comment Aimee broke the point of her pencil. She dropped the useless instrument wearily. Last night Mr. Peabody had commented, for the umpteenth time, on her marital status. And Margo was always telling her that what she needed was a man in her life. Now this. "Matt, why is everyone suddenly so interested in my love life?"

"I don't know. Maybe it's been a slow week, Aimee. C'mon," he coaxed her. "What's a few hours going to hurt?"

But Aimee wasn't about to make it easy on him. "Matt, I thought we'd come to an understanding about Phyl's and your matchmaking efforts."

"Yeah," he admitted ruefully, "we did."

"So?" She glanced up from her desk to see Margo watching her intently. Aimee deliberately rotated her chair, presenting Margo with her back, and lowered her voice. "What happened?"

"This is different," Matt insisted.

"Why?"

There was a pause, as if he were deliberating whether or not to give her an answer. "Because Montgomery asked me to arrange it."

The phone slid out of Aimee's fingers and the spiral beige cord caught on her shoulder. She recovered the receiver and pressed it back to her ear.

"*He* asked you to arrange it?" It seemed incredible. Wayne didn't strike Aimee as a man who would need or want someone to set up a date for him. All he'd have to do was to make his availability known and in no time he'd be booked up for the next month. What could he want with her?

"Way to go, Aimee," Margo said in a pseudo whisper.

Aimee waved her hand in an attempt to silence her. She could see several of the other agents observing her curiously. She shut her eyes. This was getting worse and worse. Her nervous feeling returned. Wayne was really determined. Well, she had handled determined men before.

"Yeah, he asked," Matt was saying. "Last night, right after we left your house."

Aimee still found it hard to believe. "If he wanted to go out with me, why didn't he just come right out and ask? He doesn't strike me as the shy, retiring type."

"He probably didn't come right out and ask because I warned him about you."

Now, what did *that* mean? Aimee wondered. "You make me sound like Hester Prynne in *The Scarlet Letter.*"

Matt chuckled. "You're more like Rebecca of Sunnybrook Farm."

Aimee didn't like the Goody Two-shoes image, though she had to admit it basically fit. "Rebecca was a child. I'm—" she hesitated before continuing "—older."

"Age has nothing to do with this. It's your attitude."

"What's wrong with my attitude?"

Matt sighed. "Aimee, I love you like a sister, so I can say this. You live like a vestal virgin."

"Vestal virgins don't have daughters," she retorted, a warning edge in her voice. Why didn't everyone just let her live her life the way she wanted to?

"Come to the party, Aimee. What's it gonna hurt?"

She didn't know. But she had a feeling it would. Somehow she knew that if she went to dinner tomorrow night at Matt's house, escorted by the tall blond fireman, her life would never be quite the same.

Matt prompted her, "You'll eat, you'll talk, you'll laugh a little." He obviously interpreted her silence for capitulation.

"Matt," she tried again.

"Okay, so you don't have to laugh. It's not mandatory. But this isn't anything you haven't done before, right? Do it for me, Aimee. Phyl will be fit to be tied if you don't come."

Aimee brightened at the image of Phyl and Matt tied to a stake. It had possibilities....

Okay, calm down, she chided herself. Matt's right. It'll be okay.

Aimee wound the phone cord around her finger. "Speaking of being tied, I promised you that I would draw and quarter you the next time this happened."

"Yeah, as a matter of fact you did."

She felt a smile growing despite herself. "You don't sound very worried."

"I'm not. You were always squeamish about blood. Remember bio class and the frog?"

Aimee shuddered at the mere mention of the incident.

"Are you going to come?"

She'd made Matt suffer long enough, Aimee decided. "Yes."

He laughed, pleased. "Good girl."

Woman, Matt, I'm a woman, she thought as she hung up.

And women didn't need their lives orchestrated for

them. She'd attend Phyllis's dinner party and that would be that. There was no reason why she should fear that this date wouldn't go the way all her other arranged "dates" had gone.

She glanced up to see Margo's knowing smile.

And then again, a little healthy fear never hurt anyone, Aimee amended.

Wayne drove up to Aimee's place. Nestled in the tree-lined cul-de-sac, the two-story house of honey-colored wood and light blue stucco looked warm and inviting. It suited her, he decided.

He was early. He cut the engine and sat there a moment. This was a first for him. He'd never before had anyone act as a go-between for him. He'd never had to. But then, he'd never met that special someone before.

He wondered if he was being foolish. Aimee was bound to find out sooner or later that he'd had this date arranged. But foolish or not, he was a man who went with his instincts, and his instincts told him there was something about this lady. He owed it to himself to find out if it was true.

He would rather have gone the direct route. But after what Matt had said, he was afraid that if he'd asked her out, she would have turned him down. And he had a feeling that this lady was too important to let slip away due to any tactical errors on his part.

He saw the curtain in the window of the house across the street being lifted. Someone was watching him.

"Better get out of the car, Wayne, before some well-intentioned neighbor reports you to the police for loitering," he muttered to himself.

He got out and closed the door behind him. He saw the neighbor whom Aimee had accused of having reported the fire. The gentleman was standing out in front of his house, pruning a begonia bush. At least, he was holding a cutting tool within a foot of the closest bush.

Wayne nodded at the man casually. It might have been his imagination, but the old man seemed to peer at him intently over the tops of his glasses.

The woman certainly had a lot of guardian angels, he mused as he walked up the curved brick path.

She met him at the door. Somehow he'd known she wasn't the type to keep him cooling his heels in the living room for half an hour before she made a dramatic entrance.

He liked what she was wearing. It was a simple royal-blue dress made of something soft and airy. Blue looked good on her. Burlap, he suddenly decided, would probably have looked good on her.

"Looks pretty terrific, doesn't she?" Aimee's little girl asked, popping up at her mother's elbow. She was nibbling a potato chip, her eyes intent on Wayne and his reaction.

Aimee shook her head. "Down, Heather. You're not selling Girl Scout cookies," she murmured.

Wayne grinned. "She's certainly sold me. You look lovely," he told Aimee warmly, then turned toward

Heather. "Hi, I'm Wayne Montgomery." He extended his hand to her. "We met at the fire."

Heather took the offered hand, pleased at this display of adult treatment. "I'm Heather."

She looked like a smaller version of her mother but without the wary humor about her mouth and eyes, Wayne thought, taking an instant liking to Heather.

Aimee smiled wryly. Well, he's certainly won Heather over, she thought, noting her daughter's beaming smile.

"Now, then." Aimee turned toward Heather and smoothed down the collar of the girl's blouse. She felt oddly unsettled by Wayne's compliment and needed to be doing something with her hands. Actually, she felt unsettled by Wayne, who looked entirely too good in his silk shirt, gray slacks and navy sports coat. He cut a very impressive figure. It wasn't wasted on Heather, if the size of her eyes were any indication, Aimee thought. Her little girl was growing up.

She realized that Heather was waiting for her to continue with her statement. "I know it's Friday night, but I don't want you staying up any later than eleven o'clock." She raised her brows for emphasis. "Okay?"

Heather gave her a huge smile. "Sure."

"That was too easily won," Aimee decided out loud. "Cynthia?" Aimee called into the family room over Heather's head. "Tie her to her bed if she tries to stay up past eleven." She swung back around and faced Wayne, her heart beating a tad harder than it was supposed to. "All right, Lancelot, let's sally forth." And then, to prove to herself that this was going to be nothing more than a pleasant evening, she took his arm.

With his free hand, he curved his fingers around her elbow. Aimee felt an uncustomary little thrill that had absolutely no place in her life.

"Shall we take the direct route?" Wayne was saying to her. "Or would you like me to slay a dragon on the way?"

At least he has a sense of humor, she thought. "Whatever is easiest for you," she answered lightly, then stopped short as she spied the car. "Fire-engine red, huh?" She grinned.

He held the door open for her. "You can take the boy out of the fireman, but you can't take the fireman out of the boy."

Aimee saw the way he was looking at her legs as she held up her skirt to enter the car. Excitement bubbled up inside her. So she was flattered, she chided herself. It was only natural, right? No big deal.

She waited until he slid in on his side before she responded to his comment. "Did the boy always want to be a fireman?"

He smiled. "Ever since I got my first fire truck, at the age of five."

"Dedicated." She tried not to think about how close she was sitting to him, bucket seats notwithstanding. His presence seemed to fill every inch of the car. As he started the engine and pulled away, she pressed a button and the window rolled down. She needed air to dissipate the scent of his cologne—it wasn't strong, just far too sexy.

"No," he quipped, "I just wanted to ride in a fire truck."

She chuckled. He could laugh at himself. She liked that.

Aimee's laugh wound into his senses. It was low, throaty, and he found it incredibly seductive.

"As long as there's a reason," she said.

Was she just making small talk, or was this an important clue to her personality? "Does there always have to be a reason?" he asked casually.

"Somewhere down the line, yes."

He glanced at her and saw her eyes narrow slightly.

"Are we getting philosophical?" she asked.

"No," he answered honestly, "we're exploring."

Aimee shifted in her seat. "I'm not exploring, and unless you're displaced royalty, I don't think the term 'we' applies here."

He caught the fleeting look of vulnerability that crossed her face before she shut it away. It made him want to hold her, to protect her. His reaction surprised him, as did his desire to know things about her. First he was going to have to get her to trust him. Which meant going slow. But he had to be honest with her. "Not yet, anyway."

"Beg pardon?"

He glanced at her as he turned the corner. She was smiling, but he caught lines of tension about her mouth. "Just thinking out loud."

"I see." She turned to watch the road again.

"Do you mind?"

"What?" She looked back at him, lost. "Your thinking out loud?"

"No," he replied simply, "me."

That one took her breath away. Actually, yes, she answered silently, and for the life of me I don't know why.

She realized that she was squeezing the shape out of her purse. She forced herself to relax, then gazed directly at him. She smiled, hiding her thoughts. "You're going to have to narrow that down for me just a little. If you mean do I mind your clothes, your face, your being a fireman, your being a tall, blond male, the answer is no." Okay, so I'm lying, she thought. He'll never know.

"When would the answer be yes?"

She raised her chin a little. "I'm not quite sure." She thought for a moment. "I suppose it's that I don't like being manipulated."

Her accusation surprised him. "I don't manipulate."

Oh, I beg to differ there, she thought, remembering her conversation with Matt. "What do you call getting Matt to arrange a dinner party?"

So she knew, Wayne thought. He came to a stop at a red light. Though there was traffic in all three lanes, he felt as if he and Aimee were totally alone. He gave her a long, studious glance. "Clever."

"Clever?" she echoed with a short laugh.

"Otherwise we might not have gotten a chance to get

together." He saw a slight wary look enter her eyes. "I think we should get to know each other."

"Oh, you do, do you?" A warning alarm went off inside her. Maybe she'd better get things straight from the beginning. "I don't—"

"Matt told me about your husband. I'm sorry."

For a moment she remained silent, looking straight ahead. "It happened a long time ago."

"But you haven't let go," he observed, moving the car again when the light turned green.

She turned to stare at him. "Of the memory? No. I don't want to. He was a good, kind man and I loved him dearly. I've had my share of happiness," she said pointedly. "I see no reason to try for more." She felt it necessary to explain, "I go out because I enjoy people's company. There isn't any more to it than that."

Wayne wanted to pursue the matter, wanted to pull over on the side of the road and discuss it now. His quick surge of anger troubled him. What she was saying was basically sensible, so why was he taking it personally? "Nobody ever has enough happiness, Aimee," he said finally.

"That's a matter of opinion."

"Yes, I suppose it is."

Aimee was relieved that the heavy tone of the discussion had dissipated. She didn't usually lose control over the direction of the conversation like that. She'd have to be more careful in the future.

What future? her mind whispered. Her own unguarded thought left her mystified.

* * *

Aimee had always maintained that Phyllis Baron was born to give parties. While she was a fairly decent C.P.A., Phyllis was a fantastic hostess. Tonight was different, though. Aimee could tell as soon as she walked through the door that Phyllis was worried about Aimee's reaction.

A tall woman who favored swirling, colorful caftans, she'd thrown open the door on the first ring. She swept her gaze over Aimee, apparently searching for signs of annoyance, and immediately took hold of Aimee's arm. Perhaps, Aimee speculated, to immobilize it. "So nice of you, Aimee."

"Have I ever turned you down, Phyl?"

"No."

Aimee patted the woman's hand and disengaged herself. She took off her shawl. "Cherish that thought. It may all come to an end soon."

Someone in the kitchen called to Phyllis, and the woman fairly ran in the direction of her salvation. Aimee found it hard not to laugh. Maybe she was being a little hard on her friend, but this, she hoped, would cure the woman. Of meddling in Aimee's life, at any rate.

Wayne took Aimee's hand and led her into the huge family room as if he were the one who had been to the house countless times, instead of her. Aimee let him lead, telling herself she was going to enjoy the evening and forget about everything else for the time being. After all, she did need to unwind.

It wasn't a bad party as parties went. Instead of the usual three or four other people, Phyllis had invited eight couples for a buffet dinner. Phyllis, Aimee mused as she surveyed the mingling crowd, was probably hoping that with so many witnesses, Aimee wouldn't commit murder.

Actually, she would have been hard-pressed to remember when she'd had a better time in recent months. Wayne was charming. There was no other word for it, even though she tried to find one. Aimee could see why Phyllis's hopes were up.

Sorry, Phyl, it's still no go, Aimee thought as Wayne returned with her drink. Her heart had been won once, and once was enough, as far as she was concerned. She didn't want to care for another man, if for no other reason than that she would feel disloyal to Terry.

It was a warm night, and the sliding glass door that led into the backyard was open, inviting in the evening breeze, instead of relying on the on-again, off-again whoosh of artificial air. Half the couples were inside the family room; the others were outside, on the patio.

Wayne remained at her elbow the whole evening, and she had to admit that talking to him took absolutely no effort at all. He had a wealth of stories to tell her about living in Los Angeles. And he didn't seem to mind that these stories were constantly being interrupted by someone who had a question for her. As a real estate agent she knew the best stores to frequent for new furnishings, the best contractors to contact. Wayne stood it all with patience, waiting until she was through before reclaiming her attention.

A few of the women who approached her actually wanted to be closer to Wayne. They were the ones who talked to Aimee but cast appreciative glances at Wayne, who seemed oblivious to them.

Matt passed by. "Are you having a good time?" he asked for the third time.

"Yes, Matt," she answered, doing her best to hide her grin, "I am having a good time."

Matt looked up at Wayne. "Knew she would."

"Smug, isn't he?" Aimee asked Wayne.

Wayne looked at his chief, then at Aimee. "I'll answer that when he's not around."

"I've got spies all over, Montgomery. Just remember that," Matt warned him as he responded to Phyllis's call from the kitchen.

"Would you care to go outside?" Wayne asked.

Aimee laughed. "So we won't be overheard?"

He smiled into her eyes. "No, so I can look at you in the moonlight."

Okay, take a deep breath and pretend he doesn't have the sexiest mouth you've ever seen, she counseled herself as she walked ahead of him.

"They've really got a beautiful house," he observed.

The patio was completely covered with soft, twinkling lights and colored streamers that now moved restlessly in the light breeze. She pushed aside a peach streamer as she walked by. Soft music was drifting out from the stereo in the family room.

She took a sip from her drink. "I sold it to them." She always prided herself on matching the right house to the right people.

"Did you, now?" Wayne's mind was barely on his words. He was paying more attention to how her hair curled about her face, framing it like a golden halo. How the muted lights seemed to catch themselves in it, highlighting it until it looked a silvery gold. How the front of her dress rose and fell as she breathed.

He reined in his thoughts. Go slow with this one. She wasn't like the others. And he didn't want her to be.

But he did want to hold her.

Wayne put his own drink down on a nearby table. As she looked at him questioningly, he held out his hands to her.

"Shall we?" He inclined his head, indicating the music.

On the grass, inside the tiny gazebo, another couple was dancing. Or actually, Aimee amended, taking a closer look, they were holding each other and occasionally swaying slightly to the music. She saw no polite way to refuse him, and somehow she did want to know what it would be like to be held by him. The situation couldn't get any safer than this, she assured herself as she put her glass down next to his. "All right."

The situation wasn't safe. He was holding her closer than she thought he would. There was just the faintest whiff of his cologne in the air, and she could feel her blood swimming again. Aimee hesitated to put her head against his chest. One should never invite trouble, she thought. Or had she already invited it?

"I don't bite, you know," he murmured.

She looked up. "What?"

He curled one hand around her fingers, moving his other hand against the small of her back, molding her to him. "If you put your head against me and relax, I won't bite."

She liked how his smile seemed to be slightly higher on one side than the other. It took away from his perfection and added to—what? She wouldn't follow through on her thought. "I am relaxed," she insisted.

He laughed. "Marines at attention are more relaxed than you are right now."

She let out a sigh and forced herself to relax. He was right. But she didn't know what she was being tense about. This was just an average evening, spent in the company of friends and one blind date. "Better?" she asked.

She expected him to say yes. Instead, he gave her a meaningful look. "We'll work on it."

Oh, no, we won't, she thought defiantly as she rested her cheek against his chest. The warmth there made her close her eyes for a moment, giving herself up to a dreamy sensation that filled her.

He was almost a head taller than she was, but her body seemed to fit into his very naturally. Too naturally. She was relieved when the music was over.

"It's been a while since I danced," she said, suddenly searching for something to say, something to break the spell she was drifting into. "I'm afraid I'm a little rusty."

He gazed down into her face. "We could do it again."

He hadn't released his hold on her, and she wished he would; being in his arms was far too comfortable. "No, one's my limit."

"Which is why you're a little rusty." The next song started and he began to dance again. She had no choice but to follow.

Chapter 4

It was getting late. Two of the couples had already left, and Aimee decided that it was time to go.

"I had a very nice time, Phyllis," Aimee told her. Despite the fact that she was talking to Phyllis, Aimee was very aware of the strong hands that brushed lightly against her bare shoulders as Wayne slipped her shawl into place. Her smile became forced as she tensed her entire body in an effort to restrain a shudder.

Phyllis looked from Aimee to Wayne, beaming at the couple with the air of a woman who had accomplished what she had set out to do. "I just knew you would have a good time."

"Phyllis." Aimee lowered her voice and curled her forefinger, thinking that if she didn't squelch this, rumors of her engagement would be circulating before dawn.

Phyllis, wide-eyed with anticipation, bent her head as she moved in closer. "What?" she breathed.

"Don't issue the wedding invitations just yet." With that, Aimee turned toward a very amused-looking Wayne. "Shall we go?"

Wayne felt the brisk, cool night air chill the front of his shirt. It was the kind of night that invited lovers to stroll along aimlessly and share their dreams. Wayne turned to Aimee to suggest that they walk awhile before heading home. But remembering her earlier comment about the late hour, he contented himself with taking her arm and strolling down the block to where he'd parked the car. "Does this kind of thing happen to you often?" He nodded toward Phyllis, who stood in the open doorway, watching them leave.

Aimee tried not to think about his hand on her arm, about his skin touching hers. "Matchmaking?" Wayne nodded. "Often enough, I'm afraid. There's just something about an unattached woman that brings out the Cupid instinct in her married friends."

"Unattached men suffer the same fate." They stopped as they reached his car. "This is my third dinner at Phyllis's."

Aimee raised a protesting finger to point out the difference. "Ah, but you asked for this."

He unlocked the door and held it open for her. As she slid into her seat, he bent down. His face was inches from hers. "Yes, I did."

Aimee's breath caught in her throat as her stomach quivered. It was a sign of vulnerability, a sign that would have had her running for the hills had she not thought that it had to be something else. It *couldn't* be what she was thinking. It had happened to her only once before.

She looked away into the night—anywhere but into his eyes. Then, calling herself a coward, she forced her eyes to meet his. They were warm and green and did strange things to the roots of her hair and the tips of her fingers. She had to ask. "Why?"

Wayne ran his fingers gently along the hollow of her cheek. "Because I want to get to know you, Aimee Greer." There was a promise in every whispered syllable, she thought. "Get to know you very, very well. And I want you to get to know me."

For a moment they said nothing. Aimee wondered if Napoleon had felt just this way when he had first sighted Waterloo. Anticipation, excitement, fear, all danced through her veins.

And then she found her voice. "I'm not averse to getting to know people, Wayne." Why couldn't she draw her gaze away from his mouth? Why was she growing so inexplicably warm on such a cool evening? "I know a great many people. Some might even say I'm a people person." She congratulated herself on her poised, neutral answer.

If he didn't move away now, Wayne thought, he was going to give in to the overwhelming desire to kiss her.

Abruptly, he stood up straight and closed the door for her. "Then we won't have any trouble."

"Trouble?" Aimee asked as he got in.

He slid his seat belt into place. "Getting started."

"On what?" Her voice rose a little on the second word. She wasn't at all sure they were still talking about the same thing.

As he pulled away from the curb, Wayne flashed her a smile that was both boyish and sensual.

How had he managed to pull that off? she wondered. He seemed endearing and dangerous at the same time.

"On getting to know each other."

And just what did he mean by that? Was he planning on pulling over on the side of the road the first chance he got? Was she going to have to fight him off?

She sneaked a glance at him. No, he wasn't the octopus type. Somehow she knew that about him, and it occurred to her that she sensed a lot of things about him that she shouldn't.

Like the fact that he spelled trouble.

They'd ridden in silence for a few minutes when Aimee heard a strange pop pierce the night air. Suddenly the car was swerving all over the road.

Her seat-belt harness bit into her shoulder and the strap across her lap became rigid, imprisoning her as the car swerved first in one direction, then in another. She threw her hands against the dashboard to brace her. She heard Wayne mutter a curse as he fought for control of the car.

Several heart-stopping moments later they skidded to a halt, one wheel up on the curb. Beyond the sidewalk lay a lonely golf course, utterly deserted and in darkness.

Aimee let out a long sigh of relief. She pushed her hair back from her face, then turned to look at Wayne. "Do you charge extra for this?"

He laughed shortly. "Not usually."

She saw that he was still gripping the wheel. His fingers slid off as he scanned her body quickly and said, "Are you all right?"

She liked the concern in his voice. It made her feel...special. She offered him a reassuring smile. "I've been worse. Heather enjoys dragging me on the Shock Wave ride at Magic Mountain."

"No kidding?" He unbuckled his seat belt. "That's one of my favorite rides."

Aimee unstrapped herself. "It figures. Next time you can take her."

"All right," he said slowly, "I will."

The tone of his voice brought her back to reality. What was she *saying?* What next time? The accident had muddled her mind for a moment, made her feel closer to him than she really was, she decided. The best thing would be to pretend nothing had been said. For convenience's sake, she grasped at the first bit of conversation that came to her head.

"What happened?" she asked, though she knew full well what the problem was.

"I think we have a flat." Wayne got out to survey the damage.

Aimee was right behind him. "It's the left front one."

He gave her an amused look, then walked toward the left tire.

Aimee looked around at the lonely stretch of road. The golf course was tucked in between two residential developments, and traffic at this hour was next to non-existent. It was the perfect place to pull over and snare some private moments, she mused.

She shook her head as she looked over the damaged tire. "Most men would try running out of gas instead of blowing out a tire," she commented wryly.

"Small potatoes," he quipped. He stripped off his jacket and flung it over the hood of the car. "I go for the grandstand play." He began to roll up his sleeves.

"So I see." She noticed the expression on his face. "Why are you frowning?" The answer suddenly dawned on her. "No spare?" How far would they have to walk? She tried to gauge the distance to the next gas station. At least two miles down the road, if not three. Her high-heeled sandals were new, and her feet already ached.

"Oh, I've got a spare all right," he said.

"Then what's wrong?"

"I've never changed a tire before," he admitted reluctantly.

She laughed, oddly reassured that he wasn't afraid to admit his shortcomings. Then, for his benefit, she made a vain effort to wipe the smile off her face.

"'Small potatoes'," she said, echoing his words. She held out her hand expectantly, palm up. "Give me the keys to your trunk."

Game, he dropped them into her hand, then watched to see what she would do.

Aimee walked around the back and opened the trunk. "Goodness, you're neat." She could see nothing in the trunk but a pair of running shoes.

Following her, he looked over her shoulder. "Why? What does your trunk look like?"

"Like I just bought out an entire floor of a department store," she confessed as she raised a rubber mat on the floor of the trunk. "I hate unpacking things."

Beneath the mat lay a brand-new spare tire. The unopened box containing the jack was nestled off to the side. She motioned toward the tire. "Well, let's get cracking."

When he took out the tire, she hefted the box with the jack and went around to the front of the car. She deposited the box on the ground with a thud and put her hand on Wayne's shoulder. "Have no fear, Wayne," she teased him, "I'm going to talk you through this. I'll be with you every step of the way."

He eyed the tire and then her. "Changed a lot of tires in your time?"

She gave him a smug look. "My dad was a mechanic." She tossed her shawl on top of his jacket. "I could rebuild this car if I had to."

"Now, that I'd like to see."

She didn't know what possessed her, but she winked and said, "Play your cards right and someday you might." Now, why had she said that?

She walked to the passenger side and leaned through the open window.

"Are you going to coach me from inside the car?" he asked.

Her head bobbed out. "Wise guy. I'm looking for a flashlight." She narrowed her eyes at him suspiciously, one hand on the glove compartment. "You do carry a flashlight with you, don't you?"

He gave her what amounted to a sheepish grin. "It's a pen light."

She pulled it out, then looked it over critically. "Obviously for small emergencies only." She crossed back to him. "Okay, Mr. Fireman, let's get your feet wet." She crouched, aiming the tiny stream of light at the hubcap. Wayne was still standing. "Well, what are you waiting for? A royal invitation?" She indicated the space next to her. "Get down here."

He saluted and crouched. "Yes, ma'am."

"That's more like it. Now, the first thing you have to do is jack up the car." With her foot, she pushed the jack box toward him.

"I knew that," he muttered, opening the box. He pulled out the jack and placed it under the car.

"So far, so good."

He gave her a disparaging look. "You make a wonderful cheering section." With the full moon highlighting her face, he saw her eyes shine with amusement. He wondered what they'd look like shining with desire. He promised himself to find out.

"I try." She waited until the left tire was raised off the ground. "Next, pry off the hubcap." He did and the meshed covering clattered as it landed on the road.

"Now comes the muscle part. Taking off the lug nuts." She directed the beam of light to the first of four. He picked up the only tool in the box that seemed appropriate. Aimee looked at the tool disapprovingly. It was straight, with only one fitting, instead of the star-shaped one she carried in her car.

Wayne turned the tool around in his hand, seeing nothing wrong. "What's the matter?"

"It doesn't give you enough torque. If this were my car, we'd have a better lug wrench to work with."

He toyed with fitting the tire iron over the first nut. "If this were your car, it probably wouldn't dare have a flat." He gave her a very warm, disarming look. "About now we'd probably be back at your house, necking in the garage."

She turned the light toward his face to see whether he was kidding or not, then redirected it back to the lug nut. "I wouldn't bet on that if I were you."

The look on his face faded into an intimate one that unsettled her. "No, you might not," he said cheerfully, "but I would."

She pressed her lips together in an effort to contain

a smile that refused to be beaten down. "Rather sure of yourself, aren't you?"

He braced himself as he tried to turn the tool. The lug nut held fast. "Not sure of myself. Sure of the situation." His forearms tensed.

She watched his muscles strain as he worked, and she felt an itch in her fingertips. She forced her mind back to the conversation. "What situation?"

He let the tool drop for a moment. "Oh, there's a current between us, Aimee Greer. Things are meant to happen." She opened her mouth to protest, but he continued. "I'm not sure what, but *something* is going to happen." He picked up the tool and strained against the stubborn lug nut again.

"What's going to happen is that you're probably going to wind up with a hernia." She fished a handkerchief out of her purse and wiped his brow.

Wayne started to take the handkerchief from her, then seemed to think better of it. He smiled his thanks.

Aimee wadded up the handkerchief and dropped it back in her purse. She couldn't shake the impression that she had just done something far more intimate than she had intended to. Back to the car, Aimee—quick. "Machine-tightened lug nuts can be brutal."

"Got any better ideas?" he asked hopefully.

"Not at the moment."

He sighed. "I was afraid of that."

"The sooner you get it done, the sooner we'll be back on the road," she said.

"You make a great dictator, you know that?"

She grinned. "Yeah, so I've been told."

Wayne had an urge to kiss her grin away. With a jerk the lug nut came loose. He leaned back and sat down, cross-legged, on the road.

"One down, three to go," Aimee said cheerfully, aiming the light on the second nut.

"You can be downright depressing when you want to be."

"Part of my charm. Work, Montgomery."

He rotated his shoulder, working it to dissipate a cramp. "Now you sound like Matt."

She laughed at that. "I was around him enough when I was growing up."

Wayne nodded as he struggled with the second lug nut. "So he told me."

"What else did he tell you about me?"

Wayne cast a mischievous look in her direction. "Someday maybe I'll let you know."

There's not going to be a someday for us, Wayne Montgomery, she thought. I can't afford for there to be.

The second nut came loose. Within fifteen minutes the other two were off. Wayne sat on the ground, catching his breath.

Taking pity on him, Aimee rose and rolled the tire over to him. She saw him gaze at the smear of dirt across her skirt and she read his apologetic expression. She shrugged. "It'll wash out."

Wayne knew of half a dozen women who would

have thrown a fit over getting dirty. Hell, he thought, they would have thrown a fit over having to wait while he changed the tire. Aimee was something else. He was almost glad that the blowout had happened.

They were on the road again within half an hour of the incident, both slightly the worse for wear. Wayne saw that her hair had come undone in several places and she hadn't bothered to repin the escaped strands. She looked adorable, even with the smudge of dirt on her cheek. Maybe because of it, he mused.

He pulled into her driveway. "Well, we made it." He cut the engine but made no attempt to get out. "Thanks to you."

For some reason Aimee thought the interior of the car suddenly felt very small. She had trouble catching her breath. "You would have figured it out sooner or later."

"I would, but it wouldn't have been nearly as much fun."

"You're easily entertained," she quipped.

He placed his hand over hers. "With the right person."

Uh-oh, I know that look, she thought. Time to call it a night. "That's what they all say," she said lightly, reclaiming her hand. She opened her own door and stepped out of the car.

When they mounted the two cement steps to her front door, though, she found that she didn't really *want* to call it a night. To her own fascination and unease, she realized she wanted to invite him in. To be with him.

She felt a pull toward him that she hadn't experienced since...since Terry.

The idea sent a chill through her.

Wayne saw the curtain go down over her face, which had been so open, so full of laughter, only a moment before. He wanted her to invite him in. He wanted to understand the reasons for the sudden change. He wanted to come in to prolong the evening, to just sit next to her. The feeling of just wanting to be with someone for no reason at all was entirely new to him, and he examined it carefully, a little uneasily.

"Well—" Aimee put out her hand "—it's been a very interesting evening, Wayne, and I have to admit that I enjoyed myself." She grinned impishly. "Especially the tire part. I know a lot of men who would have tried to take advantage of the situation. You were a thorough gentleman throughout the whole evening."

It wasn't quite the way he wanted to have her think of him, he thought wryly. "I'm not that thorough a gentleman."

Before she could comment, he had her in his arms. Sounds began buzzing in her ears as soon as his lips touched hers. This wasn't what she wanted, yet it was what she'd been anticipating all evening.

Although gently delivered, it wasn't a gentle kiss. It was a ruthless one. It robbed her of her shield, of her belief that no one could ever stir her but Terry.

She was in an utter panic even as she reveled in the sensation.

He pressed her against him ever so lightly, craving the feeling of her body against his, yet knowing that she couldn't be pushed. She had to be coaxed.

It was enough for now to just taste her, to hold her.

The hands that she had placed against his chest as a hurried barrier now slipped upward onto his shoulders. She rose to her toes, like a flower seeking the first rays of light after being in the dark for so long.

He was the first to draw away, from necessity rather than anything else. Something was happening, something more than he had actually bargained for. He had to explore this new development carefully. There was a strange ache within him that hadn't been there before. In laying a trap, he was in danger of being caught himself. And he wanted to maintain control; it was best to be in control when heading toward uncharted waters.

Aimee felt both bereft and relieved at the separation. They stood regarding each other in silence for a moment.

"I'd better go in," she said, fishing for her key. Damn, her hand was trembling. She shoved it into her purse so that he wouldn't notice.

"I can get that for you." His hand was on her purse, but she pulled it back out of reach.

"You worked hard enough this evening," she said a bit too quickly. "I'll do it."

He shrugged and let her. She was retreating, he thought as he walked back to his car. Well, he could accept that for the moment. He hadn't expected things to go in a forward pattern completely. There was a crack in her armor that just might be large enough for him to sneak in.

Aimee heard Wayne's car pull away as she let herself in. She had exactly three seconds to dwell on what had just happened before Emmett shuffled forward, meeting her in the foyer. "About time you got in." He surveyed the grease on her dress and face. "What in Sam Hill happened to you?"

She tried to sound nonchalant and thanked God that Emmett hadn't seen Wayne kiss her. That would start him on a roll that would work its way into the middle of next week. "We got a flat tire, and I helped him change it." She looked around. "Where's Cynthia?"

He jerked his thumb in the direction of his own house. "Got a call from her husband on my phone two hours ago. I offered to take her place while she talked." He shrugged. "She never came back." He looked at Aimee and smiled. "Flat tire, eh?" He chuckled. "In my day it was running out of gas."

She walked into the kitchen to wash her hands. As she turned the faucet on, she realized she must have gotten grease on Wayne's shirt when he kissed her. He'd probably say something about wearing her brand the next time he saw her. No, there wasn't going to be a next time. "You, Emmett, will never run out of gas."

He willingly accepted the compliment with a nod. "I slow down every now and then."

"Not so's you'd notice." She pretended to be occupied with drying her hands.

Emmett peered at her over the tops of his glasses. "You're changing the topic."

She gave him a challenging smile. "Yes, I am."

"Had that good a time, eh?"

She began to walk back to the foyer, hoping he'd take the hint. For once, he did. "It was all right."

"I heard you humming."

She realized she had been. It was the melody of a song she and Wayne had danced to. She had to get hold of herself.

"People hum," she said with a trace of defiance, opening the door for him.

"Yes, they do," he agreed. "Especially when they're happy."

"I've got a terrific daughter, a good career and a wonderful neighbor who minds his own business." She patted his cheek. "Why shouldn't I be happy?"

"No reason in the world." Emmett eased himself out the front door, eyes twinkling. "By the way, your lipstick's mussed." His chuckle sounded almost like a cackle.

Aimee put her hand to her lips, closing the door harder than she'd meant to. Shutting Emmett's smirk out of her mind, she went upstairs and peered into Heather's room. A new rock song vibrated through the air. Heather was asleep.

Aimee leaned in the doorway, her mind on Emmett's

last comment. "And that's not the only thing that's mussed," she murmured under her breath.

Her conscience was. She had to admit it. This was a date, the first real one she'd had since Terry had died. All the other times she had gone out, it was as friends, no matter what her date had thought or planned.

This time it was different. This time she'd come away from the evening aware of herself not as a friend, not as a mother, but as a woman. He'd made her remember a woman's longings. He'd opened a door that she had firmly shut six years ago.

"Damn you, Wayne Montgomery."

Chapter 5

Aimee was on her knees, wrestling with paper on the kitchen wall. She glanced at Heather, who stood on top of the blue-gray tiled counter next to the sink, her bare toes curled. She was listlessly scraping off a segment of smoke-damaged wallpaper.

Heather was not what Aimee would call a morning person. It normally took her an hour to get oriented and to speak beyond monosyllabic grunts.

"Hey, you went out with that fireman last night," Heather suddenly remembered.

Knowing what was coming, Aimee didn't look up but ran the scraper across a stubborn section of wallpaper. She had been crouching for twenty minutes and could feel the ache in the back of her legs getting worse.

"What was he like?" Heather prodded her eagerly.

Aimee decided she'd been happier with Heather's monosyllables. "Like any other man." She left it at that. Heather wouldn't understand about the electric current that seemed to have run between her and Wayne last night. Why should she? Aimee didn't fully understand it herself.

She rose, massaging one calf. As she rubbed, she surveyed her daughter's work, shaking her head. "Put a little elbow grease into it, Heather."

Heather's face had a strange, dreamy expression Aimee had never seen before. "Oh, I dunno. He seemed pretty sick to me."

Aimee smiled. Sick. The word as Heather used it had the opposite of the conventional meaning. It meant fantastic. It was funny how each generation had a new language, she thought. Her mother had probably had the same problem with her. Except, she thought, her mother had never attempted to break the language barrier. Not that her mother wasn't a good woman, but Aimee's inability to communicate with her mother was in part responsible for making Aimee want to maintain open lines with Heather at all costs.

And it was costing her now, she thought wryly, tucking several wayward strands of hair under the blue hair band she had pushed onto her hair. "No," Aimee decided aloud, "he was more on the rad side."

Heather stopped and looked down at her mother. "Huh?"

Aimee laughed. "Just language from another era, my love." She went back to work.

Heather crouched until her face was level with her mother's. "You gonna see him again?"

"I imagine I'll run into him here or there," Aimee said nonchalantly. "Greenfield's not that large yet."

"No," Heather said impatiently. "I mean *see* him. Like on a date."

Putting two hands to the sandpaper, Aimee began to rub furiously. "Nope."

Heather jumped down from the counter. "Why not?"

Aimee dropped the sandpaper, leaned her shoulder against the wall and faced her daughter. "Because, my darling precocious daughter," she said, "Mr. Wayne Montgomery has romance on his mind." Aimee could almost see the thoughts going through Heather's head.

"Isn't that good?"

Aimee rose. Time for a break. "Good for him. Bad for me." She flexed her fingers, then rinsed them under the faucet. "I'm not interested in romance."

"How come?"

"Because—" Aimee ruffled her daughter's hair "—I had a very wonderful romance with your father, and that's enough for me." She took a long sip out of a soda can, then put it back into the refrigerator.

Heather frowned, confused. "But—"

Aimee put her arm around Heather and redirected her attention to the spot where Heather had ceased to work. "What's not enough is the work we've put into this kitchen. Heather, you've got to work a little faster at this, or we'll never finish it. Today's the only time I have to do this."

Reluctantly, Heather climbed back onto the countertop and picked up her scraper. But instead of working, she looked down at Aimee. "Mom?"

Aimee was back on her knees again, sanding. "Yes?"

Heather seemed to weigh her words. "If you were married, would you still have to work?"

"Has Mr. Peabody been talking to you?"

Heather shrugged as she got back to work. "Well, I did hear him say that if you had a husband earning a living, you'd have more time to devote to things." She stopped and looked down at her mother again. "You wouldn't have to worry about providing for me."

"Come down here," Aimee said quietly, pointing to the floor. Heather did as she was told, and Aimee put her arms around her daughter and hugged her close. "Hey, kid, I *like* worrying about providing for you. You're what's important to me." She smiled at her daughter as she brushed back the silky, straight blond hair. "Now, no more of this kind of talk, okay? It's been us two girls—"

"Women."

Aimee bit back a laugh. "Women for a long time, and we've been doing just great. With the possible exception of wallpapering."

The phone rang. Aimee pointed up at the wall. "Keep working."

It was a client with a myriad of questions. No sooner had she put down the phone than it rang again.

And again.

It was days like today that made her wish she were in some other business. If Terry were still alive—

Aimee immediately put a halt to her train of thought. Terry wasn't alive, and wishing wasn't going to make it so. She'd schooled herself a long time ago to be grateful for having shared the time she had with him. A lot of people went an entire lifetime without knowing the comfort of having someone to love who loved them back.

She felt the familiar ache in her throat and chest as she thought of her husband and then shut it away. She refused to feel sorry for herself. She'd had happiness, and now she had Heather. What more could she ask for?

"Hey, Aimee," Margo greeted her the next morning as she deposited both a cup of coffee and herself on a corner of Aimee's desk. "What's on your mind?"

Aimee gratefully accepted the coffee cup that Margo offered. "What do you mean?"

"You barely made Boyce's Monday-morning tea party, although I can understand your wanting to miss it. And then you were obviously daydreaming while he recited his usual rah-rah speech about getting out there and selling, selling, selling."

Had she been that obvious? Aimee wondered. She hated to be caught napping. "I've got a lot of things on my mind, Margo."

Aimee glanced down at a photograph of one of the

newer houses she was listing. She had to make up her mind which listing she would hold an open house in on Wednesday. She should have already gotten in contact with the owners. The kitchen had taken much longer than she'd anticipated. There were still some yellow paint streaks on her left hand that she hadn't been able to get rid of. At least it matched her dress, she thought with a smile.

She realized that Margo was studying her.

"What sort of things have you had on your mind?" Then, like a flash, Margo seemed to understand. "Oh, yeah, I forgot."

Aimee raised a brow. "Forgot what?"

Margo's eyes were mischievous as she looked down at Aimee. "How did the party go?"

"Party?" Aimee framed the word in utter innocence.

"The one that gorgeous hunk was taking you to."

Aimee did her best to be nonchalant. "Oh, that party." Under pain of torture she wouldn't have admitted to Margo that she'd dreamed of Wayne again. She'd woken up in the middle of the night, shaken and upset. He had no right to be in her thoughts, and there wasn't any room for him in her life.

"Yeah, that party." Margo leaned forward. "How was it?"

Aimee glanced up into Margo's penetrating gaze. "It was fine."

Margo pressed on. "How was *he?*"

Aimee gritted her teeth. "He was fine, too."

Margo waved her hand, indicating that she wanted her to elaborate. "Put a little meat on it, Aimee."

Aimee sighed and put the report down. "There's nothing to tell. We went to the party. We talked. We danced. He took me home."

"And?"

Aimee shrugged. "And he left."

Margo leaned so far forward she almost spilled coffee on Aimee's desk. "Did he kiss you?"

Aimee didn't answer.

"Aha," Margo said in triumph, garnering a few looks from the other agents in the room as she did so.

There was no use denying it, Aimee knew. She wished for once that the phone would ring. Margo had a big heart, but there were times when Aimee sincerely wished the older woman would focus her attention on someone else. "So?" Aimee said defensively.

"So, what was it like?"

"He's a very nice kisser, Margo." She felt she owed Wayne that.

Margo beamed. "And you're going to see him again."

"And I'm not going to see him again," Aimee answered firmly.

Margo looked at her as if she had just sprouted another head. "Why?"

"Because he's a nice kisser," Aimee explained patiently.

"You're running away because you're physically attracted to him."

Aimee saw that she wasn't going to get any work done. "Margo, don't you have listings to see to?"

"They'll keep." Margo waved at her own desk. Her tone grew motherly. "I don't think you should let this opportunity get by. You're a cute kid, Aimee, but you're not getting any younger."

"Thanks."

Margo put down her cup and took Aimee's hand. "No, I mean if you meet a great-looking guy and you're physically attracted to each other—"

"Margo," Aimee warned her.

"Hey," she said expansively, "physical attraction's important, Aimee. There's absolutely no point in planning a future with Mr. Nice Guy if you don't have trouble breathing when you're around him."

Margo had managed to depict the exact feeling Aimee had experienced the night before last, and Aimee felt uncomfortable. "You're describing the effects of smog drifting in, not romance."

"You're going to fight this, aren't you?"

For the first time since the discussion had opened, Aimee grinned at her. "You'd better believe it."

Margo let go of her hand and placed her own against her forehead dramatically. "And she was led, kicking and screaming, into paradise."

Aimee shook her head. "You're incorrigible."

"I'm right."

"Right about what?" said a new voice.

Margo looked over her shoulder to see Boyce, the office manager, looking down his nose at her.

Recovering easily, Margo eased her ample form off Aimee's desk. "I'm right about to look over my listings," she answered cheerfully.

"Commendable, in light of what we just discussed at the meeting," the manager said with a sour expression. "We can't let the Albert Agency get ahead of us." He turned his eyes on Aimee. "Aimee, there's a client to see you in my office."

She looked at him, wondering what was going on. Usually, clients walked into the office and whichever agent got there first claimed them as his own.

"Well, let me go and meet him." Aimee rose, smoothing her skirt.

"According to him, you've already met." He looked toward his office.

Aimee's stomach tightened.

A tall blond man in a suit walked toward them. Wayne. Aimee felt surprised and puzzled and just a little annoyed.

"He came in earlier," Boyce continued, "when you weren't here, and although Foley was on duty, the client told him he would only work with you. Must be your charm." There was a touch of sarcasm in his words, which Aimee chose to ignore.

"Must be." She watched Wayne approach. Did somebody up there hate her? she wondered.

She waited until Boyce had left the area before she spoke.

"What are you *doing* here?" she whispered, hoping Margo wouldn't hear.

Wayne looked at her innocently. "I want to buy a house."

"No, you don't."

"Yes," he said firmly. "I do."

She stared at him. "Since when?"

He nodded toward the chair next to her desk. "Do you mind?"

"Go right ahead."

He eased his large frame onto the chair. "Since I decided to stay here permanently. Buying a house is a good investment." He grinned as he leaned in closer toward her. "Or hadn't you heard?"

Aimee slowly sat down, her gaze never leaving Wayne's face. "I've heard, all right. Why didn't you say anything the other night about wanting to buy a house?" Aimee felt herself being hemmed in by him, and she didn't like it. She liked even less the feeling of excitement that his presence generated within her.

"The other night was pleasure. This is business."

"You're giving me the business, all right."

There was pure mischief around his mouth. Suddenly, she recalled the feel of his lips on hers and began counting to ten.

"Lady, you ain't seen nothin' yet."

She tried to ignore the strange tingling sensation that was licking at her nerve endings.

"All right," she said. If he was going to go through this elaborate charade, she'd oblige him. "Just what are you in the market for?" she challenged him, pulling out her book of listings.

"A three-bedroom house ought to do it."

She began thumbing through the book, though she knew everything that was up for sale. She made a notation in the margin. "Planning on having guests?"

He smiled placidly. "A man likes to be prepared."

"Well, there are several houses I could show you when you have the time."

He put his hand in between the pages just as she began to close the book. Their eyes met. Aimee told herself not to look away, no matter what the condition of her stomach. A person had to face dilemmas head-on. And he was a definite dilemma.

"I have the time," he said. "Today's my day off."

Lucky me, Aimee thought, resigning herself to her fate. "All right, Mr. Montgomery." She pulled her purse out of the bottom right drawer. "Let's go house hunting." She led the way out to the parking lot.

They stopped beside her car. Wayne put his hands on her shoulders, and she stiffened.

"I thought a lot about Saturday night," he said. She turned her head, and he thought he saw a flash of fear in her eyes.

"Yes, it was a nice party." She shivered involuntarily as he slid his hands down her arms before releasing her.

Wayne got into the car. "I wasn't talking about the party."

"No?" She seated herself and turned on the ignition. "I was," she said briskly.

"I was talking about kissing you." His voice was low and it pulsed along her skin. It was as if she wasn't wearing any clothing at all, she thought in despair.

She made no move to pull out of the parking space. Instead, she turned and looked him squarely in the eye. "Wayne, don't misunderstand. I think you're a very nice man." *I also think you're a threatening man.*

He ran his hand along her arm. The smattering of tiny hairs began to stand up as her flesh tightened. "That's a start."

She deliberately pulled her arm back. "No, that's a finish. It doesn't go anywhere from here."

"Why not?"

He sounded infuriatingly patient. She struggled to find words that normally came so easily to her when she had to explain her position to other men. She realized it was more difficult for her now because he wasn't like any other man—wherein lay her problem. "Because I won't let it."

"At the risk of sounding repetitive, why not?"

"Because I had something very special once and I lost it. And I'm never, ever, going to be in that position again. I won't let myself."

"Maybe you won't be able to stop it."

"I can if it doesn't start." She cut the engine. "Maybe someone else had better show you the houses, if you're even interested in a house." She started to get out.

He took her wrist, and though he held it lightly, she couldn't get herself to pull away. She was held in place not just by his words but by something within her that longed for him to make a case.

"Yes, I am interested in a house. I'm tired of living in an apartment. I've lived in apartments all my life. I want something to call my own. I've been rootless far too long." He let go of her hand and waited.

She dropped her other hand from the door handle.

She studied him for a long moment, feeling empathy for him despite herself. She knew what it was like to want to belong. She'd been that way before she had married Terry. She restarted the car. "All right, I'll show you a house."

One house turned into two and then five. And then seventeen. She spent the entire day with him. Several times during the course of the day, positive that he was just using this as an excuse to be with her, she referred to the bedroom in a previous house or the family room in another, just to hear his response. To her surprise, he'd kept all seventeen floor plans straight.

Maybe he was serious after all.

Wearily, she walked away from the seventeenth house. She got into the car and sat, hands clenched on the wheel, as Wayne got into her car. Enough was enough, she thought. "Just what is it you're looking for, Wayne?"

"I'm not sure."

That's obvious, she thought.

"But I'll know it when I see it."

Though she was flattered that he sought this unique way of getting her attention, she was tired of games. She had a job to concentrate on. She got an idea. "Okay." She flashed him a grin. "I think I have just the house for you."

This'll put him in his place, she promised herself.

Wayne leaned back in his seat, his fingers laced behind his head. So far the day had gone pretty well, he reflected. They had gotten to talk a little over the quick lunch they'd had, and he'd been able to subtly probe her mind, learn her tastes in things. The more he knew about her, the more they seemed in tune. In a way, he found that a little disturbing, even though things were going his way. He couldn't help having a moment's doubt in questioning whether maybe he wasn't getting in over his head.

He wondered what she had on her mind. Her grin, the first he had seen all day, highlighted her face and reassured him that going forward was a very good idea....

Aimee drove down a tree-lined dirt road, one of the last existing unpaved streets in Greenfield. She stopped her car in a long, winding driveway and waited to hear his protest of disapproval. The Maxwell mansion wasn't really a mansion; it had gained its pretentious name from one of its previous owners. It was a rambling three-story Victorian house that needed a lot of understanding and a lot of work.

Well, he hadn't liked anything else that she'd shown him, she told herself. He deserved to be faced with this. She herself liked the old house. It had been empty ever since she was a child. The property had been in Louisa Maxwell's family for over four generations with only a caretaker looking out for it. Now her great-grandson Collier wanted to sell it—for nearly any price. There had been no takers, and since the property was away from the heart of the city, the planning commission hadn't yet cast its eye in the direction of the "mansion." Aimee wanted to find it an owner before that happened. She wanted its charm to be preserved, and if she could have, she would have bought it herself.

To her surprise, Wayne didn't ask her what she thought she was doing. He got out of the car.

Aimee got out on her side and followed him. As a young girl she'd played here with her friends, and she had a fond place in her heart for the house, which had borne witness to so much history.

Wayne climbed the front steps and then stopped, waiting for her to catch up.

Aimee hung back, waiting for him to say something.

"Do you have the key to this one?" He tapped the lockbox on the front door.

It wasn't what she'd expected him to say. She fished

the key out of her purse. "Are you serious?" she asked as she joined him on the front porch.

"Why shouldn't I be?"

"It doesn't strike me as the type of house someone like you would be looking for."

"And just what kind of a person am I?" They stepped into the dusty interior of the hundred-year-old house. The drapes were drawn, and it was dark, even with the cracks of sunlight breaking in.

Aimee groped around for the light switch. "A person who tends toward sleek red sports cars." A chandelier suddenly came to life, casting shadows as well as brightness. As a child, she had thought of it as spooky. Now it was just charming.

"I'm not one-dimensional," he said, and put his hand on her shoulder as if to guide her in.

"No," she had to admit, "I'm beginning to realize you're full of surprises." She noticed he was looking past her head and grinning. "What?" She turned.

"A spiral staircase." He left her side to investigate.

"It's not too sturdy," she called after him.

He heard it creak in protest under his foot. "Nothing a little work couldn't fix."

She stared at him. Did he really like this house? And why did the possibility please her so much?

She followed him through the house, rather than the other way around. He explored the various rooms and their collection of covered furniture with the enthusiasm of a young boy having found a pirate's cave.

When they walked into the master bedroom, he asked, "How long has it been empty?"

"About twenty years," she told him. "The furniture belonged to Louisa Maxwell. She died of a broken heart, so the story goes, right here by the window—" she walked over to it "—waiting for her husband to come home from the war. World War II."

Aimee couldn't help looking out. What had the woman thought of as she had sat here day after day, waiting…? Aimee turned away from the window, only to bump against Wayne. For a moment she felt an urge to put her arms around him, to have him hold her and make her sadness go away.

"There's a lot of romance in this old house, I guess," he said, his voice husky.

She cleared her throat. "Something like that." How could he see into her mind like that? She drew away from him, away from the window.

Wayne glanced out, then back at Aimee. He crossed the room and joined her. "Well, I think I've seen enough."

"Thank goodness." She turned to leave.

At the bottom of the stairs, he asked her, "Do you always react this way to your clients?"

"Most clients don't ask to see eighteen houses."

She drove back to the agency and parked next to his sports car. She glanced at her watch. "Well, I think Heather's done without me long enough."

He didn't get out. "How about dinner tonight?"

"No." She shifted in her seat, needing to say no

because she wanted to say yes so much. "I really do have to be getting home. Besides, there's some work I have to finish up."

She felt both relief and disappointment as he got out of the car, saying, "Fine." He rested his arms on the rolled-down window. "I'll just stop at the store and then meet you at your place."

"Excuse me?"

"Any objections to a home-cooked meal?"

She began to demur. "I'm really not up to making anything elabor—"

"I meant me."

"You cook?"

"Why does that surprise you?"

She shrugged. "I don't know. At this point I guess nothing about you should."

He shook his head and gave her a smile that seeped into Aimee's senses. She felt a slight measure of panic at not being able to disentangle herself from him. Worse yet, she really did like his company. Her reaction fed her confusion, which annoyed her. She'd always known what her next step would be.

Until now.

"All right, I accept your offer."

"Great." He straightened up. "And then while I'm working, you and I can discuss the price on the Maxwell house."

Her eyes grew wide. "You want to buy it?"

"Absolutely."

Chapter 6

He looked as if he belonged in her kitchen. Heaven help her, he looked as if he came with the kitchen, as if he fit right into her life.

But he doesn't, and he won't, she thought fiercely.

Aimee sat on the far stool at the bar that ran the length of the tiled counter. Nibbling on a carrot stick, she watched as he prepared dinner. Carrying two bags of groceries, he'd arrived at her house half an hour after she had.

She glanced at her daughter, who was at his elbow, totally enraptured. Heather had just gotten home when Aimee arrived. Every day after school, Heather took the bus to the Y, where she engaged in different activities until five o'clock, when Cynthia or Emmett brought her home. It wasn't the way Aimee would have liked things to be, but she was grateful that arrangements could be so easily made and that Heather was with people she liked and trusted.

Still, Aimee would have liked to give Heather a traditional home, one with a mom who wasn't running off at all hours to close deals, dragging in next-door neighbors to stay with her so that she wouldn't be alone.

Then why don't you do something about it? she asked herself.

I am, a defiant voice answered in her head. I'm buying lottery tickets.

The other alternative was to get married, and she'd sooner trust her chances to the whimsy of Lady Luck than again risk loving someone and then losing him.

Wayne was totally involved with his preparations, yet he sensed her staring at him. He looked up, and their eyes met and held. He felt that there was a momentary awkwardness to the situation. To his relief the intensity passed quickly, and he went back to chopping onions as he answered a question Heather asked.

Aimee looked down at his hands. They were large and strong and, she was certain, infinitely capable when it came to all duties that were involved in fire fighting. They didn't, however, look like the kind of hands that could chop onions or create a soufflé. Yet he was doing it.

He was also winning Heather over. Usually she was indifferent to the men who came to the house to escort Aimee to one thing or another. Wayne, it seemed, was a different matter. It probably had something to do, Aimee mused, with the fact that Heather was growing up. Wayne, handsome, charming, friendly, was just the type for Heather to practice her budding talents on.

He seemed to be tolerating it quite well.

He seemed to be doing a lot of things quite well, Aimee thought almost resentfully. He hadn't really been out of her mind since she had met him. And, she thought in utter dismay, she had known him for only a few days. She wasn't like this. What was going on? Maybe it was overwork.

Maybe, a part of her thought, it's loneliness.

She crunched her carrot stick, determined to banish the notion. How could she be lonely? She was so busy that she had to schedule in time for breathing.

She stood up and saw Wayne raise his eyes to her questioningly.

"Where did you learn to cook?"

"At home, when I got tired of eating cornflakes and toast."

Heather agreed. "Does sound a little tiresome."

Tiresome? Aimee thought. Where had Heather picked that word up? Wayne was certainly having an effect on her little girl. The next thing she knew, Heather would be giving up baseball.

Wayne mixed the onions in with the other ingredients. "Especially day in, day out."

Heather watched, utterly fascinated—as if, Aimee thought, she had never seen a meal prepared before.

"Didn't your mom cook for you?" Heather asked.

Aimee crossed over to the center of activity. "Heather, we don't pry."

"Friends don't *pry*," Wayne informed Aimee, earning Heather's undying love. "They take an interest."

"Sometimes," Aimee muttered, knowing when she was outnumbered, "too strong an interest."

Heather seemed not to hear her. "Well," she asked, "didn't she?"

"I'm afraid my mom died when I was very young."

He stated the words matter-of-factly, Aimee noted.

"Oh," Heather said. "Like my dad."

Wayne nodded, smiling kindly. "Like your dad. My dad was always away on business, and my older brothers weren't really interested in anything but junk food—and girls." He laughed as he added the last two words.

"So, what did you do?" Heather pressed him.

He began to grease the bottom of the soufflé dish. "I got a cookbook and taught myself how to cook."

"Gee." Heather was all eagerness. "Can you teach me?"

"Heather!" Aimee cried. Heather had never asked her for any pointers, had never even expressed any interest in cooking except as a means to an end, that end being accommodating her voracious appetite.

Heather's smitten with him, she decided. Another very good reason for Aimee not to allow anything to happen between herself and Wayne. There was nothing

more intense than a young girl's first crush on an older
man, and the last thing in the world she needed was to
have Heather feel as if they were competing for the same
man.

Heather cast a rueful look at her mother. "I only
thought that maybe—"

Wayne interjected, "I wouldn't mind teaching you,
Heather." He tested the batter for consistency. "And
while I'm at it, maybe you'd like a few pointers on
pitching." He'd noticed a baseball glove and bat on the
living room sofa on his way into the kitchen.

Heather's eyes grew wide. They looked, he mused,
a lot like her mother's, only far less guarded.

"Would you?" she asked eagerly.

"Sure. Hand me the pepper." Heather couldn't get it
for him fast enough.

Aimee wondered if she could tap into Wayne's
system. She could never get Heather to move that
quickly no matter what she tried.

He tossed a dash of pepper into the bowl. "I spent a
couple of seasons playing semipro baseball," he stated.

"Wow! Why'd you stop?"

"Yes," Aimee chimed in, not quite certain if she
believed him, "why'd you stop?" She returned the
pepper to its place in the spice rack.

"Broke my pitching arm," Wayne confessed.

"Oh, gee, that must have been really rough," Heather
sympathized. She leaned her elbows on the counter,
cradling her upturned face between her hands.

She looked, Aimee thought, as if she could stay there like that forever, just worshiping him.

"At the time it was. But I got over it. The thing about life, Heather, is that you have to roll with the punches, take what comes and not let it break you." He was looking directly into Aimee's eyes.

Heather nodded sagely, and Aimee rolled her eyes.

"Say," Heather said eagerly, "would you like to come and watch me swim at the next meet?"

Okay, enough was enough, Aimee decided. "Heather, I'm sure Mr. Montgomery—"

"Wayne," he corrected her.

Aimee didn't miss a beat. "Has other things to do besides—"

"No, I don't."

Aimee sighed. Foiled again.

"If I'm not on duty," he told Heather, "I'd love to come. When is it?"

"Next Saturday."

He did a quick mental calculation. "I'm off on Saturday."

Heather clapped her hands together with enthusiasm. Aimee threw hers up in the air. Wayne caught the gesture as he poured the contents of the bowl into a soufflé dish.

"Is that surrender?" he quipped.

"That's frustration," she answered, then laughed. "Don't give up easily, do you?"

"No, I don't give up at all."

The smile he gave her warmed her and chilled her

at the same time. If trouble had a face, it was made up of broad angles and planes, with green eyes, a mouth made too wide by smiling and a noble nose. It was a handsome, fascinating face. But Aimee had a feeling that even if it hadn't been, she would have been attracted to it. Attracted to him.

It had to stop. Now.

She was spared from having to make a comment by the telephone. She stepped into the living room, where she could still see what was going on in the kitchen. "Aimee Greer speaking."

"Ms. Greer, this is Hollander, Amos Hollander," the voice on the other end said. "I've decided to take the Coopers up on their offer."

One house down, a hundred to go. "That's a wise choice, Mr. Hollander, and I'm sure the Coopers will be delighted."

"If you don't mind, I'd like to sign the papers now."

"You're afraid of changing your mind again," she guessed, her voice kind.

"No," the gruff voice on the other end of the line contradicted her. "I'm afraid of Angela changing her mind. It's taken me this long to convince her that this deal is the best we're going to get. She's still muttering about leaving behind the kids' handprints in the driveway."

"I'm sure we can find a way to have you take them with you, if that's what you'd really like," Aimee said soothingly, trying to think of someone who could handle this job for her.

"No, that's not what *I* want. She's so damn sentimental, though.... You will be right over, won't you?"

"As soon as I can get the Coopers," she promised.

She rang off and searched through her book for the Coopers' phone number. In the background she heard Heather laughing with Wayne and felt a pang of— what?

She felt left out.

A commission could do a lot to alleviate that, she promised herself. She'd be splitting the fee with Foley, but three percent of the selling price could still go a long way to make her stop worrying about her own mortgage payments for a while.

"Mrs. Cooper?" she said to the voice that answered the phone. "I have wonderful news. The Hollanders have decided to take your offer." She waited as the woman shouted the news to her husband, envying her that simple act of sharing.

C'mon, Aimee, what's gotten into you? she chided herself. All this escalated matchmaking has taken a toll on your mind. It's time to clear Wayne out of here.

As soon as she made arrangements to meet the couple at the Hollanders' house, she set about doing just that.

"I'm afraid I can't stay," she announced as she walked back into the kitchen.

"Aw, Mom," Heather groaned.

She gave her daughter an apologetic look, then smiled. "You won't be groaning 'Aw, Mom' when I get you that ten-speed bike you've been drooling over."

"Really?"

"Really. Now, I'll get Cynthia over to stay with you. I shouldn't be long." She turned to Wayne, for some reason half-dreading what she was going to say. "I'm afraid this can't be helped."

She expected him to look put out or, at the very least, grumble about all the trouble he'd gone to.

"I understand."

"Could you try not being so perfect?" she complained.

He broke into a grin. "Would it help if I stomped and yelled and had a tantrum?"

She pretended to think it over. "That might do for openers."

"I'm afraid it'd make the soufflé fall." He took off his apron and draped it over the back of a stool. "Could I take a rain check on the tantrum?" He followed her into the living room.

Aimee picked up her purse. "And I'll take one on the dinner."

He leaned against the doorjamb, folding his arms in front of him. "No need to do that. It's in the oven already. I'll just stick around until it's done and take it out—"

"You don't have to do that." There was that panic again, she thought.

"No, but I want to. Aimee, you have to eat." He ran his hand along her side, and she tried not to flinch. A burst of flares followed the path of his hand.

Why couldn't he just leave her alone, or at least stop touching her when she least expected it? She felt both a physical and an emotional pull toward him—she knew Margo would be breaking out the champagne at that admission—and she had to put the brakes on right now, before the situation got worse or anything happened.

The problem was there were too many people on Wayne's side. Even her own daughter.

Even herself.

He's offering you friendship, Aimee. You're just overreacting.

She wasn't convinced of that. Not with the way her limbs felt when he looked at her.

"Well, right now," she told him, "I have to go on automatic pilot, no matter how hungry I am."

He walked her to the door. "The soufflé will be waiting for you when you get back."

She closed the door, then muttered, "Good. Just as long as you're not."

She got hold of Cynthia and asked her to stay with Heather, warning her that Wayne would be there, as well—but only for a short while, she hastened to add. Cynthia seemed to take it all in stride and promised to be right over.

The business arrangement took a lot longer than she had planned. After a long, complicated transaction, Aimee watched with a sense of satisfaction and a great deal of weariness as, at the stroke of eleven, the papers were all signed and ready to make their way to a local escrow company. Her stomach complained loudly of neglect as she eased herself behind the wheel of her car.

The Coopers were at her side before she could close the door. "We can't thank you enough," Mrs. Cooper said, clutching her hand.

Aimee smiled. "The look on your face is thanks enough. That and a bit of dinner." She put her hand over her stomach.

Mr. Cooper leaned over, one hand on his wife's shoulder. "What do you say we go down to Baxter's and celebrate?"

Aimee smiled. "No, thanks. I've got a soufflé waiting for me. I'd better call it a night. You two go down and celebrate for me."

Immensely satisfied both with the transaction and with her part in helping the Coopers get their first house, she drove home wearily.

But her sleepy state completely vanished when, as the automatic garage door yawned open and she pulled inside, she passed Wayne's car on the way.

"What the devil is he still doing here?"

She got out and slammed the car door behind her. Didn't the man know how to take no for an answer?

"Obviously not," she muttered, jabbing her key into the lock. Wayne and Heather were in the living room, on either side of the glass-topped coffee table. Between them was a Monopoly board.

Wayne looked up at Aimee as she walked into the

room. His lips parted in a broad smile. "I haven't played this since I was a kid."

Since she thought that he was playing the game only as a ploy to stay until she returned, she expected him to abruptly call an end to the game now. Instead, he turned his attention back to the game board and rolled the dice. In desperation, she turned toward her daughter.

"Heather, it's late."

"We're almost finished, Mom," Heather pleaded.

"Did you get the sale?" Wayne asked without looking up.

"Yes, I closed the deal." She couldn't keep the pride out of her voice.

"Then look at this as a celebration game."

Aimee gave up and walked into the adjoining family room. She found Emmett there, comfortably arranged in a recliner, hands folded across his stomach. He was sound asleep.

She touched his shoulder, and his eyes opened reluctantly.

"Fine babysitter you are," she remarked.

"Don't have to be." Emmett jerked his thumb toward the living room. "He's watching her."

"Speaking of watching, where's Cynthia?"

"One of her girlfriends dropped by to take her to the movies. She doesn't get out enough with Ray away."

"You're an old softie," Aimee said fondly.

He struggled out of the chair. "I'm not an old anything." He raised his chest. "I'm just now reaching my prime." He tapped his temple. "Age. It's all in the mind. And my mind's as young as ever." He gave her a significant look. "So are my eyes."

"Meaning?"

"Meaning that I think you've finally met your match, Aimee Greer. This one," he said with a look toward the living room, "you won't be making a friend out of."

She was afraid he was right, but she wasn't about to agree. "I assume you can let yourself out."

"Always have before." He began to walk to the front door.

"Emmett?"

He stopped and looked over his shoulder. "Yeah?"

Her voice was warm. "Thanks for coming by."

"Anytime. Now, get yourself some dinner. The soufflé's dang good. He's quite a catch."

"For someone," she agreed. "But not for me."

"Never knew you to be a fool, Aimee," Emmett said loudly enough for her to hear as he left the room.

"I'm not," she whispered to herself as she walked into the kitchen. "Only fools leave themselves open to the same pain twice."

With that she went to sample the now famous soufflé.

Chapter 7

"Couldn't I stay up just a little longer today?" Heather begged.

Aimee put away the Monopoly box. "Any longer and it'll be tomorrow, not today." She eyed Heather expectantly.

With great reluctance, Heather rose looking at Wayne hopefully. "I guess we'll have to play again some other time."

"Count on it."

Heather brightened visibly. She rose on her toes and lightly brushed her lips against her mother's cheek. "G'night, Mom."

"She will hold you to it, you know," Aimee told Wayne.

Wayne unfolded his long legs and stood up, pushing

his hands into his back pockets. "I never say anything I don't mean."

She wasn't altogether sure she liked the sound of that. It held a promise as well as a threat. "Admirable quality," Aimee grumbled as she followed Heather to the staircase. "I'll just be a few minutes," she promised.

He nodded complacently. "I'll be here."

"That's what I'm afraid of," she muttered.

Heather overheard and looked at her, confused. Aimee pointed toward the stairs. Heather shrugged and raced up to her room.

Aimee entered Heather's bedroom just as she pulled her shapeless nightgown from under her pillow. "Is he going to stay overnight?" Heather asked with the wide-eyed innocence only a ten-year-old could manage.

"No."

"Oh. I was just wondering."

"Well, don't." Was Heather growing up that fast?

"Allison Baker's mom sometimes has guests stay overnight."

It was Aimee's turn to say, "Oh." She felt a little foolish at her defensiveness. She stuffed Heather's castoffs into the hamper. "Wayne has his own home to go to. Mrs. Baker's guests were out-of-towners."

Relieved that Heather wasn't growing up quite as fast as she had feared, Aimee gave her a hug as a head and arms emerged from inside the nightgown.

"Good night, princess."

Heather bounced into bed and pulled up her covers.

"G'night, Mom." She was reaching for the radio dial when Aimee closed the door behind her.

Aimee stood for a moment at the top of the stairs, all her attention focused on what was waiting for her in the living room. She was psyching herself up to face Wayne, knowing by now that he wasn't the type to just fade away gracefully.

Gracefully. The word brought back the memory of the dance they'd shared. She'd experienced a thrill in his arms, but that was only natural, wasn't it? He was a good-looking man, and after all, she wasn't exactly frozen in suspended animation.

She'd felt frozen after Terry had died, but slowly she'd come around. Feelings and desires were only a natural part of life. And now, after all this time, *they* seemed to be coming around, as well. It was up to her to be in control. And she was up to it—hadn't she controlled everything else in her life for the past six years?

She squared her shoulders and descended the stairs. Her courage lasted as far as the living room. Pep talks were terrific, as long as she wasn't in his presence. When she was near him, all her well-thought-out resolutions seemed to dissolve like morning dew in the face of the sun.

He was sitting on the sofa, looking very comfortable, as if he'd been coming here for years. She damned him for it and for the nervous flutter she felt overtaking her.

His smile invited her to sit beside him. She sank into the chair opposite him and saw him raise a brow slightly.

"It's my favorite chair," she explained. She realized

she was sitting on the edge and shifted back, attempting to look relaxed. She told herself she was being silly. Why was she so tense?

Wayne got up and went behind her chair. He put his hand on her shoulder. "Any stiffer and a doctor would say that rigor mortis had set in."

She twisted around in her seat to look up at him. "What?"

His eyes were kind. "Don't be afraid of me, Aimee," he said softly.

She raised her chin. "I'm not afraid of you."

His expression grew thoughtful, and he let his hand drop. "Yes, you are."

She shrugged. "Okay, maybe just a little."

"Why?"

She rose. "It's such a warm night. Why don't we go out and sit on the patio?"

"All right." He moved to put his arm around her, but she moved quickly and left space between them. At first he looked surprised, then he grinned broadly and laughed. Another man's ego would have been hurt, she mused. Instead, he reacted with humor. It showed a core of inner strength, of easy self-confidence.

When he joined her in the kitchen, she was arranging two tall glasses on a tray. "Is iced tea all right?" she asked a bit too brightly. She took a pitcher out of the refrigerator and hoisted it for his approval.

"Anything wet would be fine." He glanced down at the hand that held the pitcher. "New fashion?"

She followed the direction of his gaze and saw the three long yellow streaks of paint that had refused to wash away. "I painted the kitchen yesterday."

He looked at the wall over the sink and recalled the peeling wallpaper. "Did a good job."

"I paint—you cook. We all do what we have to."

After a pause he said, "Yes, we do."

She had the feeling that he meant something far more complex than she did.

Wayne watched as she bustled around the kitchen, her movements barely masking the edgy energy he knew was inside her. She was a woman a man wouldn't mind coming home to, a woman to warm his heart and his bed. He wondered what she would say if she knew what he was thinking.

Probably head straight for the hills, he guessed. He had to admit that his thoughts made him a little nervous, as well. As odd as it seemed, it was unnerving to finally find what he thought he'd been searching for all along. Was she really what he needed, or was his desire for a stable home life making him lose his perspective?

Aimee was putting a straw into each glass.

He nodded at the tray. "You don't have to go to any trouble, you know."

"No trouble." She picked up the tray and walked toward the back door. "Besides, you made the soufflé. Did I tell you that it was excellent?"

"No."

"It was excellent." She stopped at the door. "Emmett says he thinks you're quite a catch."

He opened the screen door for her. She stepped out, and he followed. The screen groaned as he slid it closed once again.

Wayne laughed. "A catch, eh? That's not what my older brothers would say."

Aimee set the tray on the small glass table next to the swing seat, and Wayne sat and waited to see if she'd join him. There was just enough room for two on the swing. A friendly two.

For a moment she hesitated, then, seeing the challenge in his eyes, she sat down. She picked up the iced-tea glass with two hands and held it between them as if for protection. She toyed with the straw before she took a drink. "How much older are your brothers?"

She had soft, delicate hands, Wayne noticed. Even with the yellow streaks. He wanted to know what it was like to have those hands touching him, caressing him.... He kept his thoughts from his eyes. "Will's seven year's older, and Wyatt's ten."

"All *W*s?"

He nodded. "My father tended to stick to a good thing when he thought he had it. That's why he stayed with his job for so long, waiting for that big break that never happened. I lived with Willy Loman for years before I ever read *Death of a Salesman*."

"Oh, I'm sorry."

He saw genuine sympathy, not pity, in her eyes, and

it unlocked another layer in his own heart. "Don't be. It was—" he searched for the right word "—an education. I swore that failure would never happen to me. It made me grow up tough." He laughed self-depreciatively. "You have to be tough when you yourself are all the family you have to lean on." He picked up the glass and held his drink rather than tasted it, remembering all those years.

Aimee was thinking that she shouldn't be asking any more questions. The more she knew, the closer it brought him to her. She was supposed to be putting up barriers, not taking them down. "Where are your brothers now?"

"Wyatt's got a farm in Indiana. Raises kids, mostly." He took a sip. "Hey, this is pretty good."

"Just plain iced tea." She liked the sound of compliments from him and knew she shouldn't.

"Will took after Pop," he continued. "He's a salesman. On the road most of the time. Except that he's doing well." He put the glass back on the tray. "Your turn."

His thigh was against hers, and it was difficult for Aimee to think of anything except the steamy, weak feeling that was slowly making its way through her entire body. "My turn?" she echoed.

"Yes." Unable to resist, he moved closer to her, casually draping his arm around her shoulders.

The casualness frightened her most of all. It seemed so natural for him to hold her, to kiss her, to— No! That path led to things she couldn't touch anymore.

"I've told you about me. Now I want you to tell me about you."

She stirred her iced tea again. She was beginning to feel very warm and took a long drink. "I would have thought that Matt told you everything you'd want to hear."

His fingers lightly grazed her temple, moving wisps of silken blond hair away. Aimee's breath grew short when he replied, "He only whetted my appetite."

She didn't respond, except to clutch her glass more tightly. He saw the wary look in her eyes.

His breath touched her cheek. "I've already told you, you don't have anything to fear from me."

"Don't I?" The words escaped before she could stop them.

He took the glass from her hands and put it down on the table. Gently, he turned her head toward him, touching her so lightly that she almost melted into his arms. She could feel her heart thudding against her ribs.

"One should never fear affection," he stated.

She drew back. It took a supreme act of willpower. "One should if one's smart." She tried hard to distance herself from him emotionally. It was a struggle she felt destined to lose. "I had a wonderful marriage, Wayne. The only thing wrong with it was that it ended all too abruptly."

Wayne began to get a vague inkling of exactly what he was up against. She was afraid to enter into a relationship with him because of his job, he decided. She was afraid of him dying. "The good don't always die young." He grinned beguilingly. "Sometimes we stick around to a ripe old age."

Something made her continue. Something made her want him to understand. "Until I can have that in writing, I'm afraid—"

He wouldn't let her finish. He took her hand, though she resisted. "Well, what about you?"

What was he trying to say? she wondered. "What about me?"

"Well…" He stroked the inside of her hand. "Maybe if we entered a relationship I'd harbor the same concerns about you—"

She wanted her hand back. It was all too easy to fantasize those caresses moving along her body instead of her hand. It didn't help her thought processes, and she felt that it was important that she be logical. "There's no reason to harbor anything about me," she protested.

"But I could. Can you guarantee that you'll be around for a long time?"

"For one thing, I don't fight fires."

"But you cross streets," he pointed out.

"I fail to see—"

"And drive a car," he continued.

"Yes, but—"

"And eat canned goods."

"Canned goods!" she echoed, incredulous.

He was unruffled by her reaction. "You could be

run over by a car, die in a car crash or contract a fatal case of botulism."

She yanked her hand free and folded her arms across her chest. "You're reaching," she scoffed.

"Only for you."

With a firm hand he pulled her closer to him. They fit so well, she marveled. "You're not going to be graceful about this, are you?" she asked with a touch of despair.

He turned her face toward his with the crook of his finger. "Bet your bottom dollar I'm not. Not unless you're the consolation prize."

"I never thought of being any sort of prize before." Each word left her throat with great effort. His eyes held her prisoner. She lowered her gaze to his lips and felt drawn there. There was no escape.

"Start thinking," he said, then, tilting her head slightly, he lowered his mouth to hers.

The warmth of his body melted her resistance. As they kissed, she felt her blood racing, singing. She felt alive as she hadn't since…the last time he had kissed her.

Wayne pressed her to him, needing her, wanting her. Things were happening, things he hadn't fully antici-pated, things he hadn't reasoned out yet.

The taste of her mouth was so sweet he couldn't get enough. Over and over again his mouth touched hers, in a thousand different ways, igniting a thousand dif-ferent sensations within him. The word *madness* flickered through his half-dazed brain. No sane man could want someone so much. Wanting took control away, and he'd always had control before. Sitting there alone in a dark room as a child, watching shadowy characters flicker across a television screen, he'd promised himself that when he reached legal age, he would take control of his own life and never lose it. Yet here he was, handing over the reins to her, letting her be master of his fate.

It would be madness not to, madness to relinquish this dark, sweet happiness that was clawing at him.

He ached to touch her, to peel back the bright yellow dress and brush his palms lightly against her breasts. He ached to claim her as his own. He knew it was too soon. A little of his control seeped back into him.

Aimee wanted him to touch her, to satisfy the desires that had suddenly sprung, in full bloom, back to her. She felt tears searing her eyes. No, not again, please, not again. I can't go through this again.

Taking a deep breath, feeling as if she were tearing herself apart, she pushed him back, whispering hoarsely, "No."

He fought to steady his breathing. His hands still burned to touch her. Anger and frustration warred within him. He managed to hold them both at bay. But he needed to hold her, to reassure them both that this was right, that it was real. He moved to reach for her. "Aimee," he said softly.

Aimee sprang to her feet. "No," she repeated, half

defiant, half pleading. She swung around to face him. "There's no room in my heart for anyone else. I have loved and do love all the people I intend to love. Please—" she begged him with her eyes "—try to understand. I loved Terry with all my heart. When he died, I thought I died. And I did, for a while. But I had a daughter to think of, so I kept on. I will not—do you hear me?—will not go through all that anguish again."

"What makes you think I'm going to die?"

She put her hands to her face, trying to steady her breath. "What makes you think you're not? I don't see any *S* on your chest for Superman."

He put his arms around her. "You didn't look close enough."

Aimee broke away, her fists clenched at her sides. "It's not funny."

"No, it's sad," he agreed. This time he made no move to hold her. "Very sad that you'd let something special get away just because you're a coward."

"All right." She threw up her hands. "I'm a coward. So sue me."

"Aimee, I want to love you, slowly, gently, the way you deserve."

His words brought visions to her and made her ache. She pressed her lips together, searching for courage. It wasn't fair. It just wasn't fair.

"Aimee."

He took a step toward her, but she backed away, hating herself for it.

"I'm very attracted to you. Like you, I'm scared as hell. I've told myself all my life that this was what I wanted, something steady, something pure and wonderful. Now that it's here, I'm afraid." He saw her eyes widen. "Yes, I'm afraid, but unlike you, I'm not going to run away from it until I've explored from every angle what's happening here between us, until I've made damn sure that I'm not throwing away the chance of a lifetime just because I was shaking in my boots."

"It's just physical attraction," she said.

"It's a hell of a lot more than physical attraction and you know it. I like you, Aimee Greer. I like the kind of person you are. And I think you feel the same way about me."

"I—"

"Go ahead." His voice rang with suppressed anger. "Deny it."

"I like everybody," she said stubbornly.

"I'll face that crowd if I have to. I have a feeling I'll win out."

She tried to turn away, but he wouldn't let her. He placed his hands on her shoulders and made her face him. "Aimee, I'm not asking you to marry me. I'm not asking you to do anything at all except to take this thing we have one step at a time and see where it leads."

She felt tears forming again and held them back. "And I'm asking you to leave me alone."

"Sorry." He shook his head. "That's something I can't do. I don't want to look back twenty years from now, sitting in a singles' bar and saying, 'What if…?' I like to take advantage of my options."

"You hound them to death." She smiled shakily.

"That, too." He kissed her lightly, then let her go. "If fear is all that's stopping you from crossing the line that separates friendship from a healthy male-female relationship, then I intend to give you all the courage you need." He opened the screen door and stepped inside the kitchen. "Good night, Aimee."

She put her hands on her hips. He'd said he'd give her courage, she mused. "Who do you think you are, the Wizard of Oz?"

He gave her one final look over his shoulder, a whimsical smile playing on his lips. "Maybe, if that's what it takes."

He left her standing on the patio with a tray of half-empty iced-tea glasses and an exceedingly panicky feeling in the pit of her stomach.

Chapter 8

He didn't come by or call for three days. It should have made her feel happy or at least relieved, she thought. But she felt restless.

You're just waiting for the other shoe to drop, Aimee.

She knew that her reaction was a lot more complicated than that. He was acting the way she had asked him to; he was leaving her alone. And she hated it.

Actually, she thought, looking down at the rose on her desk, that wasn't entirely true. He wasn't leaving her alone. He was conducting mental warfare. And he was winning, too. He might not have shown up in the flesh for the last three days, but each morning a rose, fresh from the florist, had.

She missed him.

There was no denying it, she thought with a smile.

The transplanted L.A. fireman had set a fire in her blood. And the fire was inextinguishable, even without him there.

He was always on her mind. While talking to clients, she would suddenly get such a vivid image of his smile, so sensual, so exciting, of his eyes, so soft, so kind, that she'd lose her train of thought. More than once she'd noticed that the person she was speaking to was looking at her oddly, and she would realize she'd drifted off again. Not exactly a good way to conduct business.

But it was a hell of a way to conduct a romance. And she had a feeling that Wayne knew what he was doing to her mind.

"Wish someone would send me roses," Margo said, sighing, when she spied the latest one on Aimee's desk.

Aimee got up and deposited the rose, vase and all, on Margo's cluttered desk. The first one had gone to Heather. Yesterday's was still on her desk, still plump, still radiant, with a hint of promise to its bloom.

"Here, have one on me."

Margo grinned lecherously. "Does that go for the sender of the rose, as well?"

"Yes," Aimee snapped, planting herself back in her chair. She flashed Margo a rueful smile. "Sorry."

"Has you all tangled up inside, doesn't he?" Margo's expression was sympathetic.

Aimee put down her work and looked at Margo. Frustration creased her brow. "I don't know how to read him. When I call him a perfect gentleman, he sweeps me into his arms and kisses me." Aimee saw Margo's expression turn starry-eyed. "When I anticipate him popping out at every corner, he disappears. He doesn't fit into any pattern." She spread her hands helplessly.

Margo took hold of the rose's stem and twirled it between her thumb and forefinger. "He's unnerving you."

Aimee put her appointment book into her purse and closed it. "I'll say."

"So when's the wedding?"

"No wedding, Margo," she said firmly, and meant it. "Just a funeral—*his*—if he keeps driving me crazy."

Margo chuckled as she tucked the stem back into the vase. "You'd be a lot more convincing if your eyes didn't glow like that whenever you mention his name."

Aimee stuffed a folder into her drawer and stood up abruptly. "I have an open house to go to."

"You can run," Margo told her placidly as she got her own things together, "but you can't hide."

Aimee tossed her head. "Just watch me." She shoved open the front door.

But the next day, when she saw him open the front door to her realty office, Aimee didn't have a place to hide. Suddenly she felt nervous.

She was infinitely grateful that Margo was out showing a house and that the office was all but empty. She wished she had perfected the art of appearing nonchalant. She picked up a pen and pretended to be busy writing something. She clutched the pen so hard her thumbnail dug into her forefinger.

Go away, Wayne, she thought.

When his shadow fell across her desk, she looked up.

"Hi." He pulled up the chair next to her desk and straddled it, leaning his arms on the back.

His expression told her that he'd missed her, that he liked being here, liked just looking at her. "Hi," she answered, feeling a smile spreading across her face in response to his.

He nodded at her desk. "I see my flowers have been getting here."

"Like clockwork. People think I have a secret admirer."

"You do." He put his hand over hers. It felt warm, inviting. "But he doesn't want to stay a secret anymore."

She slipped her hand out from under his and began arranging papers on her desk into neat piles. He was the only one who had the ability to make her fidget, she mused. "I think that song won an academy award in 1953."

He grinned and took her hand again. This time she didn't pull it back.

"What do I win?" he asked.

She remembered that he called her a prize, and the word *me* bubbled up in her throat against her will. No, she had made her decision a long time ago, and she was going to stick by it. Of course, there was no point in being rude.

"That hasn't been decided yet." She looked down at

her desk. "I'm afraid I can't go out to lunch with you," she began. "I've got—"

"I didn't come to take you to lunch," he told her simply. He stroked her hand with his thumb.

"Oh." Open mouth, insert foot, she thought. "Why did you come?"

"To buy a house."

That ploy again. Well, she wasn't averse to showing him some more houses. She took out the listings book. "We've been through most of the available ones, but I can—"

He reached over and closed the book gently. "You've already shown me the house I want."

She looked at him blankly. "I did?"

"Don't you remember? The Maxwell house. We, um, didn't get a chance to talk about it that night." His smile was teasing. "But I was serious. I'm interested."

"Really?"

Watching as she nibbled on her lower lip, Wayne felt a great urge to do the same. "Really."

Aimee was incredulous. Part of her still didn't believe him, just as she hadn't when he'd originally told her that he was interested in the old house. "All right. Collier Maxwell is asking five hundred and fifty-five for it."

He seemed to roll the figure over in his head. "What do you think it's worth?"

"I'm really not supposed to tell you that." He continued to look at her, the question remaining in his eyes. She stood her ground.

He appeared to come to a decision. "I'll offer four hundred thousand."

She tilted her head. He wanted to kiss her then and there. He nearly did, but someone walked into the office just then.

"Are you sure you're new to this game?"

"I've shopped in Mexico on occasion."

"And dickered." She found it hard to visualize him haggling over the price of a piece of pottery.

"And dickered," he agreed.

Maybe he was serious, after all. Picturing him as the owner of the large, rambling house pleased her. The Maxwell house needed a loving owner, and she had no doubt in her heart that he would be just that.

And a loving husband, as well?

Stop it! she ordered herself. "I'll put your offer through today."

She turned and smiled at the couple who had entered the office. "I'll be right with you." The man nodded. He and the woman went on talking in low whispers as they looked at the various floor plans on display on the side wall. First-time buyers, Aimee thought.

Wayne rose, drawing her attention back to him. Now that the matter of the house was settled, she expected him to make some sort of attempt to see her, to take her to lunch or dinner. Instead, he began to walk nonchalantly toward the door.

"Well, give me a call when you hear anything," he said.

"Sure," she said uncertainly. What was he up to, damn him? "Um, Wayne?"

He turned, that infuriatingly sensuous smile on his lips. "Yes?"

She searched for a reason for detaining him. "Thank you for the roses."

"My pleasure."

And then he was gone.

"Now, what do you make of that?" she said aloud.

The office manager, Boyce, walked into the sales area. He saw the couple standing around, unattended, and Aimee looking at the door with a bemused expression on her face. "What did you say, Aimee?" he asked.

He startled her, but she regrouped. She crossed over to him. "I think we've just sold the Maxwell mansion."

It was worth putting up with her own uncertainties just to see the way Boyce's jaw slackened.

After that, she kept in touch with Wayne by telephone. He seemed to her to be content with that. Why hadn't he come by? It didn't make any sense. She hated things that didn't make any sense. She was still busy with her job, with Heather, with the swim meets, but there always seemed to be a part of the day when she found herself alone with her thoughts. And her thoughts were always about him.

He was driving her crazy.

She called Wayne when the Maxwells turned down his initial offer. Unfazed, he countered with a decidedly better offer, and she went back with that. They both knew that this time it would be accepted. She was finally convinced that Wayne was serious; when she called to tell him that the house was his, he sounded too pleased not to be taking this seriously.

Escrow went through amazingly fast. It seemed as if Collier Maxwell couldn't wait to be rid of the family albatross. In lightning speed, the Maxwell mansion changed hands and became the Montgomery mansion, she mused as she drove home from work.

She laughed at herself when she realized that she had attached that title to it. At the same time, she found it difficult not to still think of it as the Maxwell mansion. She had played there and Terry had kissed her there, by the eaves, for the very first time.

Terry. Aimee's hands tightened on the steering wheel as she pulled up into her driveway. She suddenly became aware of the fact that she hadn't thought about him for several days. Lately when a man's name or image had come to her, it belonged to Wayne, not Terry. She met the realization with mixed feelings.

No time to brood, she warned herself as she unlocked the front door. This was a day for celebrating. "Heather! Heather, where are you?"

Heather came down the stairs two at a time. "Right here." She was chewing on an apple. She came to an abrupt halt one step from the bottom. Heather pointed at Aimee's face with the apple. "Hey, what's up?"

She realized Heather must have noticed the happy

look on her face. Aimee dropped her purse and crossed over to Heather to give the girl a warm hug. The Maxwell house had been her listing, so the eight percent realtor's fee—almost forty thousand dollars— was all hers. "We, my girl, are going out to the finest restaurant in Greenfield and celebrating."

Heather crunched down on her apple, then asked, "How come?"

"Because today escrow closed on the Maxwell place. I sold it!" Aimee announced joyously.

"The house that Wayne bought?"

"How did you know that?" She hadn't mentioned to Heather that Wayne had made an offer, because she hadn't wanted to get her own hopes up by admitting that he was actually serious.

Heather walked into the kitchen and threw away her apple. "Wayne told me."

Aimee watched her daughter walk back to the stairs. "When did you see Wayne?"

"Today, at the fire station. He was just coming off duty."

Aimee narrowed her eyes, and Heather held both hands up innocently. "Hey, it's practically next door to the Y. I took a walk."

Aimee knew it was far less innocent than it sounded, but at the moment she was too happy to care about her daughter's matchmaking attempts. "Walking's healthy." She let the matter drop. "Get dressed. I'll see about making reservations."

Heather took two steps up the stairs, then stopped. "For three?"

"Why three?"

Heather shrugged. "Well, I think it's only fair. After all, Wayne did buy it. If he didn't, we wouldn't have anything to celebrate. Yet."

The last word was said softly, but Aimee heard it. And pretended not to. The crush she thought Heather had on Wayne had turned out to be hero worship—and an acute desire to have Wayne in the family. "I'm sure he's busy."

Aimee went to the living room and got out the yellow pages. As she casually flipped to the restaurant section, she had a feeling that the discussion wasn't over. Part of her didn't want it to be.

Heather stayed where she was. "No, he's not busy. He said he's going to be home tonight, waiting."

Aimee's head jerked up. "For what?"

Heather shrugged. "He didn't say."

Had her young daughter cooked up something with Wayne? Aimee wondered. It would be just like him to use her feelings for Heather against her. To use her feelings for *him* against her, she thought, annoyed.

Was he waiting for her to call him? No, that was ridiculous. She was letting her imagination run away with her. She eyed the phone, then looked up to see Heather watching her.

Heather gave her the thumbs-up sign and then ran up the stairs.

Aimee looked back at the phone. "Well, Heather has a point," she muttered.

No, he was leaving her alone. Let it stay that way.

You know better than that. He's doing it on purpose. He's waiting for you to call.

When hell freezes over.

Aimee picked up the phone and dialed. He answered on the first ring. Maybe he *had* been waiting.

She opened with "Heather tells me you're sitting at home, waiting."

"Yes?"

For the first time in her life Aimee wasn't sure how to deal with honesty. "I wanted to know for what."

"The sound of your voice."

His voice was smooth, low, and washed over her like warm, soothing waves. At the same time it made her long to see him.

"I thought that maybe if I played hard to get, you'd call."

Her hand tightened on the phone. "Then you miscalculated."

"Did I?"

She could hear the smile in his voice, and she wanted to wipe it off his face.

"You called, didn't you?" he was saying.

"My mistake." She started to hang up. She shouldn't have called. Just the sound of his voice was stirring up things inside of her again.

"Aimee." His voice stopped her.

She lifted the phone back up to her ear. Steady, she told herself. "What?"

"Don't hang up." His voice was soft, coaxing. Sultry. "Playing hard to get's no fun. Can I see you tonight?"

"Heather would love it."

"And you?"

She twisted the cord until it threatened to pop out of the receiver. "I'm not at liberty to say."

His tone was amused, patient. "Taking the Fifth?"

"Something like that. Heather asked me to invite you to the restaurant for our celebration."

"What are we celebrating?"

"My commission. Your buying the Maxwell mansion. Take your pick."

"How about a little of both?"

It gave her a graceful way out. "Done."

It was five now. He wanted to come right over but schooled himself to be patient. "Six o'clock too soon?"

Yes. No. Come now. "Six'll be fine."

Aimee had been to Baxter's before, but it had never seemed quite so special. With Heather sitting between them in the booth, she and Wayne talked as if they were old friends. She was surprised at how much she'd missed talking to him these past few weeks.

She sipped her white wine after Wayne made an innocuous toast to please Heather. It's happening, Aimee, she thought. You're falling for him.

If she had any sense, she'd grab Heather and run.

But, she mused as she took another sip, she was way past making any sense. Women in love seldom made any sense at all.

Oh, no, she thought in sudden despair. I don't want to love someone again. What am I going to do?

Wayne noticed a change in her expression, and although he didn't miss a word in his conversation with Heather, he wondered what had happened. And then, looking into her eyes, he thought he knew.

He raised his glass again. "To happiness. May we all find it."

Heather took a sip of her ginger ale. "Aren't you going to drink, Mom?"

"Yes, of course." Aimee picked up the goblet. "To happiness."

She met Wayne's gaze over the rim. Did they define happiness in the same way?

He insisted on paying when the check came. They argued about it all the way to Aimee's house, with Heather taking up Wayne's side.

Ever since he'd come into their lives, Aimee thought, she'd lost a little bit of Heather. She didn't know whether to be upset or to be glad that Heather had picked someone like Wayne to be attached to, if she had to be attached to someone else.

"We invited you, Wayne," Aimee insisted, adamant that he not pay for the meal.

"And as a guest, I should be humored." His voice was mild.

"Can't anyone ever tell you anything?" Aimee asked in exasperation.

There was that smile again, backed with steel. "Not if I don't want to hear it." He pulled the car up to the curb and got out.

"I suppose that means I'm in trouble." She took his hand as he helped her out of the car.

"That depends on how you define trouble," he said, and held her hand an extra few seconds.

"Six foot two, blond, with green eyes."

Wayne laughed and slipped one arm around her shoulders. The other went about Heather as she all but tumbled out of the backseat.

Once inside the house, Heather did a vanishing act, announcing that she was tired. Aimee had expected her to want to stay up in order to hang around Wayne.

"She's a pretty sharp girl," Wayne commented.

He was in the living room, lingering by the fire-place. She noticed that his dark blue suit brought out his tan. He looked better than any man had a right to. "How so?" she asked, then began to fluff the sofa pillows.

Wayne watched her hands. Her nervousness was almost imperceptible. But he had come to be attuned to a great deal about this woman. Was that what love was all about? he wondered. Noticing ordinary things and finding that they made you smile? "She knew I wanted to be alone with you and she cleared the stage."

"Great little stage clearer, my Heather." She returned

the second pillow to its place. Her hands felt empty, and she was afraid of what she might do to fill them. She longed to touch him, to run her hands along his body and convince herself that he was here, that he would always be here. It had been such a long time....

He walked over to her. She wanted to rush into his arms, yet she stood, waiting, anticipating, fearing. He fitted his arms around her and held her to him. *Home,* she thought.

Wayne kissed her forehead lightly. "Did you miss me?"

He wasn't going to leave her any pride, was he? "Must you be so direct?"

"Shortest distance between two points. I'm not ashamed to say I missed you." He cupped her cheek. "I don't want to stay away any longer."

"Wayne." Her words were soft. "One of us is going to be hurt."

He lowered his mouth to hers. "Not if we play it right."

Aimee wound her fingers into his thick hair. The bittersweet feeling that swept through her took her breath away. Yes, her mind cried, yes. She had missed him more than she thought humanly possible, certainly far more than was good for her. She knew that and yet she couldn't help herself. Later she'd look at the consequences. Right now she had to drink this in or die.

She pressed her body along the length of his as he moved his hands up and down her spine, molding her to him. She felt the heat of his desire against her, and it set off her own. If it were possible to burn for another human being, she burned for him.

When he touched the sensitive area along the sides of her breasts, she caught her breath. Knowing she should push him aside, push aside her own passion, she pressed his hand to her.

She felt so delicate Wayne was afraid of hurting her. But he couldn't pull away. With his mouth he covered her eyes, then her throat.

His blood hummed in his ears. He was afraid that if he didn't stop now, he'd make love to her right here, in her living room, and that wasn't the way he wanted to do it.

He was shaken. Never had his own control slipped so much. Never had he wanted anyone so much. And yet she belonged to someone else. To the ghost of the man whose ring she wore.

"Oh, Aimee," he murmured, pressing her head against his chest as he hugged her. He wanted to tell her that he loved her, but he knew the time wasn't right.

He didn't know what it was about her that kept reeling him in. He'd gone out with other women, women who went out of their way to make time for him in their own lives, women who didn't try to block his attentions at every turn. And he'd enjoyed those relationships. But something had been missing. Substance, quality, that mysterious something that kept attraction alive long after the initial surge. Aimee was attractive, warm and appealing, yet he had come in contact with all that before and had never felt like this.

"I don't intend to give up," he told her.

Aimee wondered whether anything had ever been so comforting as leaning her head against his chest and hearing his heart beat. "I should encourage you to," she said simply. She raised her head to look at him. "I'm too afraid."

He dropped a kiss on each of her lids, then released her. "You won't always be. And when you're not," he promised her, "I'll be there."

He left her relieved. He left her aching. Most of all, he left her confused.

Chapter 9

Aimee wished she had the ability to be in three places at the same time. Then maybe things would get done on time, she thought as she rushed around at eight the next morning. It was Saturday, and if possible, Saturday was even more hectic for her than the rest of the week.

"Heather," she called from the bottom of the stairs, one hand on the banister, "have you seen the box of heat cards?"

Heather's voice came from her room. "I think it's next to the box of heat sheets."

"Terrific," Aimee muttered. More loudly she said, "And those are?"

"I dunno."

Aimee shook her head helplessly. "Back to square one."

Wait, she thought. Last night she'd stayed up, sleepless, after Wayne had left, and she'd arranged everything for the next morning. She'd finally fallen asleep at three and, naturally, overslept. Now, where...? The family room, of course.

Before testing her deductive abilities, she decided to prod Heather one more time.

"Heather, get a move on. They're not going to keep the meet waiting for you." She strode into the family room. There they were. How could she have missed them?

"No," Heather agreed as she thundered down the stairs, a vision of perpetual motion in cutoff jeans and a T-shirt, clutching her towel and her swimsuit, "but they will hold up the meet for *you*. Nobody's going to be able to keep score if you don't turn up with the heat sheets and cards."

Aimee stacked one box on top of the other and stuffed the paper clips and rubber bands into her purse. "That's what I love—no pressure." Now, what had she done with the pencils?

She saw the open pencil box on the floor beneath the coffee table and added it to the pile. The pencils rolled from one end to the other, threatening to overflow as she hefted the entire stack of boxes.

Aimee balanced the stack as she walked toward the front door. The bell rang. "Oh, now what?" she asked irritably.

Heather was right behind her. "Maybe it's Ginny Rogers."

"Why would it be Ginny Rogers?"

"Because she said she might be by for a ride."

"Heather, we're not running a car service, too," Aimee cried in exasperation. Life at a gallop was exhilarating, but there were times… The bell rang again.

Aimee shot her daughter a look. "Two hands, Heather. I have only two hands."

Heather nodded sheepishly. "Right. Sorry."

Wanting to redeem herself, she reacted overzealously, pulling the door open so fast that she bumped into Aimee's arm. A shower of sheets, cards and pencils hit the tile. Aimee just shook her head and, with great reluctance, bent over and began to collect all the scorekeeping paraphernalia. When she looked up from her position on the floor, she saw a pair of sneakers and faded jeans molded to muscular thighs. There was no need for her to guess whom they belonged to.

Wayne crouched to her level. "Need help?"

"Nothing I can't handle," she muttered. For the first time in her life, she began to doubt her own words. Things *were* getting to be more than she could handle. She didn't need or want him here now to unsettle her any further.

Wayne scooped up a handful of pencils and dumped them into the box. "I admire your independence, but there's no shame in needing help once in a while."

"I'll try to remember that." She glanced at her watch. They had ten minutes to get to the Y. All the lights had better be green.

"Which is why I'm here," he said.

"Why *are* you here?"

Rising, Wayne pulled a long list out of his back pocket and tapped it. "There are a few questions I need to ask you." He'd remembered that at Matt's party people had seemed to regard her as a source of information, and now he was going to turn that to his own advantage. There were questions on his list that would keep her in his company all day—if he played his cards right.

Aimee stood up, hands full. The pile she held began to totter. Wayne was quick to wrap his hands around hers, reinforcing her hold on the stack. She could easily give in to the strength there, she realized, then tightened her grip as if to deny his effect on her.

"What sort of questions?"

Wayne raised his brow, waiting for her to relinquish her stack to him.

After a momentary battle of wills, Aimee surrendered the boxes to him. She walked out of the house and to her car, with Wayne right behind her. Heather brought up the rear.

Wayne continued, "Well, now that I'm a home-owner, I need to know the name of a good carpenter, a reliable plumber, what kind of vacuum cleaner I need for the rugs. And there are wooden floors in the dining room that desperately need help," he enumerated. "So I came to the best source."

Aimee opened her car trunk, which was nearly over-flowing with a multitude of bags, blankets and tools.

"You were right about your trunk. You could hold a garage sale in there," he quipped.

She eyed him. "It's not that bad."

"If you say so." Obligingly, he elbowed a paper sack out of the way and deposited the boxes into it.

Aimee closed the lid firmly and put her hand out for Wayne's list. He pulled it from his pocket again, and she gave it a quick perusal. It was a mile long. She didn't have the time to go over it with him now.

"I'm going to have to get back to you on this. Heather and I have a swim meet to get to in—" she glanced at her watch "—eight minutes, and I absolutely hate being late for anything."

"Another admirable quality."

"We'll write my testimonial later." She walked around to the driver's side. "Get in, Heather."

Giving Wayne a forlorn look, Heather got in on the passenger's side.

Wayne kept his hand on the door after he closed it for Heather, but his gaze was on Aimee. "Mind if I come along?"

She shook her head, resigned. "I had a feeling you'd ask." Aimee gestured toward the car. "Get in."

As soon as she heard her mother's answer, Heather unbuckled her seat belt. She looked positively radiant as she leaped out of the front seat and scooted into the back ahead of him. "Here, sit next to Mom."

"I love children who aren't obvious," Aimee said as she positioned herself behind the wheel.

"Oh, I don't know. I sort of like having someone on my side." He winked at Heather.

"Everyone seems to be on your side," Aimee grumbled as she started up the car. She glanced at his list, which he still held. "Even the house."

Heather did her best time that day, and, thinking about it the next evening, Aimee was certain that it was because Wayne had been there to watch her. Aimee shook her head. Heather's attachment to Wayne was something she couldn't ignore. If she were in the market for a husband—which, she told herself, she definitely wasn't—she could do a lot worse than Wayne. As a matter of fact, if she were looking for someone, she'd want him to be just like Wayne. He seemed so supportive, so easygoing, so interested in everything that was a part of her life, hers and Heather's.

No, she couldn't fall into that trap. Wayne was a very nice man, but she wasn't about to fall in love with a very nice man, no matter how much Heather liked him.

No matter how much, she thought, her mind drifting, her skin tingling, he stirred her passions. She had had passion in her life, and she had paid for it. Nothing was ever obtained in life without a payment, and she couldn't afford to pay again.

"So why are you making room on your calendar to help him fix his house?" she chided herself, staring at the different notations.

From down the hall, she could hear Heather's music

blaring. Heather, as usual, was working on her weekend homework at the last possible moment. How anyone could do their homework while their ears were falling off was beyond Aimee.

She looked back at Wayne's list. She wasn't going that far out of her way. It was no more than she'd do for anyone. Hadn't she been there for the Fennellis when the water pipe had burst in their upstairs bathroom a month after they moved in? This was nothing new, just part of her service—which was why when houses went back on the market, clients sought her out.

She was a sucker, she thought in dismay, circling next Tuesday on her calendar. A sucker for a pair of liquid green eyes that touched her soul and a smile that could have defrosted an old-fashioned refrigerator.

Admit it. This time your helpful-Hannah routine is different. This time it's downright intimate.

And it was. There was something basically intimate about helping Wayne with his house. She wanted to help him fix up the house where she had played and daydreamed hours away.

You're committing yourself to him without even realizing it, she thought. She sighed and rose, walking to the window, her hands clasped behind her back. "And pretty soon you will be committed. To an institution. Pull away *now*."

She could no more pull away than she could fly. She could see what lay ahead of her, see the anguish at the end of the road, yet she seemed to be powerless to stop it. She felt as if she were sailing off to her own doom.

"Have I told you how terrific you are to be doing all this?" Wayne asked.

He handed her a glass of white wine. It shimmered, catching the light from the fire he had just started in the fireplace in his new home. It seemed to her oddly appropriate to have a fire going, even if it was June. The air was chill, and outside, it was raining.

It was overwhelmingly cozy.

She accepted the glass. "You've told me several times." She took a long swallow. The wine made her feel warm, fluid. Or at least she thought it was the wine. "No big deal."

Wayne mused that she'd come through with flying colors. Not only had she brought landscapers, contractors and plumbers, but she'd come herself, to help when time permitted. Working with her these past few weeks had helped to convince him that the decision he found himself unconsciously making was the right one.

He set his glass aside on the rug behind him and moved closer to her. "Are you always such a do-gooder?"

If he meant to sneak up on her, he failed, she thought. But she was glad he was moving closer. Glad of it and still afraid.

She swirled the golden liquid around in her glass. Despite her headache, the lights from the fire fascinated her. He fascinated her. Maybe she'd had enough to drink.

"Always." She took another sip. Her head began to feel better. "I was raised on Donna Reed reruns." She took another swallow, bigger and healthier than the last, and the rosy glow increased.

Wayne picked up a strand of her hair and raised it to his lips. Its fragrance filled his head. She filled his head. And his heart. His eyes caught sparks of the same fire as he shook his head. "Nothing on television can take credit for creating something as wonderful as you."

She lifted the glass to her lips again, but it was empty. When had that happened?

He kissed her shoulder through her T-shirt. He burned it away.

Her breath caught in her throat. Breathe, dummy, breathe.

He curled her hair about his finger, studying her.

She stared down at his cream-colored rug, which he'd put in at her suggestion.

She looked up at him, her thoughts jumbled. Why did he find her so attractive? Why was he pursuing her when she'd let him know there was no hope? And why was he becoming so precious to her even while she erected barriers?

"I haven't been with a man since Terry died. Or before him, either." She fumbled, wondering what had possessed her to tell him that. Yet she wanted to be honest with him. She wanted him to know everything. As a friend.

"I mean, Terry was the only one. Ever." She shifted uncomfortably. "I suppose that isn't a very sophisticated thing to admit."

He raised her head until her eyes met his. "On the contrary, I find it very, very sophisticated."

He smiled at her, creating within her an infinity of emotions and feelings. For the past six years, life had been a portrait of subdued grays, browns, beiges. He created a kaleidoscope of pastels within her. He created rainbows.

"I find it endearing," he went on, and moved to kiss her lips. As he did, he tasted something wet and salty. She was crying.

"Aimee, what is it?"

"I don't want to love you, Wayne. I don't." She struggled to gain enough courage to end this. She wasn't sure anymore of what she wanted.

Maybe it was the wine that gave her courage. She didn't know. All she knew was that she was talking, telling Wayne things she'd never told anyone before. Unlocking a part of herself no one had ever known. She needed to say it, to share it. With him.

Aimee's words rushed out. "In every relationship there has to be one who loves more. In ours—Terry's and mine—it was me."

Wayne felt a pang of jealousy, but he banked it down. Gently, he stroked her hair as she spoke.

"Not that Terry was cruel to me or anything like that. I just knew that I loved him more than he loved me." She sighed, remembering. "When we were in school, I was the one who went after him. He just stood still and let it happen. After we were married, he had his work, his hobbies. I had Heather, of course, but I loved him more than I loved life itself. When he died, I thought I would, too. I didn't understand how I could make it through a single day without him in it." She raised her head, needing to see Wayne's eyes. Needing to know he understood.

"Loving him was all-absorbing, all-encompassing. And when it was over, when he was gone…" Her throat ached with tears, but she went on. "I was completely depleted. On the outside I went on—I didn't change. I doubt that anyone knew the extent of what was going on inside. Because on the inside I was devastated, hollow, only half a person." She clenched her hands in her lap. "I don't ever want that to happen again."

Wayne cupped her cheek with his hand, loving her with his eyes, with his touch. "You don't have to love me *that* much. I'm not a demanding lover."

She shook her head, her cheek rubbing against his hand. "Don't you see? I don't think I can love any other way. I'm afraid I will and I'm afraid I won't."

"That covers a lot of ground."

She took the hand that caressed her cheek and held it in both of hers. "I don't want to love you any less than I loved Terry—that wouldn't be fair to you. But I don't want to love you that way. It's too painful."

He took her into his arms and whispered into her

hair, "Then love me differently, Aimee. But just love me."

Aimee wanted to, with all her heart and soul, but there were still too many things in her way, too many feelings, so long locked away, that had to be dealt with.

"Wayne, I—"

"Shh." He kissed her words away, then held her and kept her words at bay. "Don't say anything now. We'll work it out," he promised.

But somehow she doubted it. Whatever solution he might come up with, it wouldn't blot out the memory of the pain she'd felt when she'd lost the one she'd loved the most in the whole world.

"Hey, Montgomery," Matt snapped as he walked toward the front of the fire station. Wayne was checking some equipment on the truck. "Make yourself useful." He pushed a piece of paper into Wayne's hand. "Here's a list of supplies we need from the supermarket. Take Mulkowski with you, but for God's sake keep him away from the Twinkies. The pantry's still full from his last trip to the store," he grumbled.

Wayne shoved the list into his shirt pocket. "Sure," he responded absently.

"Hey." Matt tapped Wayne's chest with the tip of his unlit cigar. "Something bothering you?"

Wayne shrugged. "No."

"It's Aimee, isn't it?"

Wayne rested his foot on the edge of the truck's rear

bumper. "Matt, it's been two months and I still can't get through to her."

Matt pursed his lips and tried to look philosophical. "Jacob toiled for Rachel for fourteen years."

Wayne swung his foot down. "You're a big help." He pushed his hands into his back pockets and began to walk away.

"You're seeing her, aren't you?" Matt's words brought him to a halt.

Wayne turned around. "You know I am."

Matt's expression indicated that he didn't see the problem. "Well, that's a hell of a lot farther than anyone else has ever gotten with her."

It was far too serious now, far too special, for him to take it as a game. "I don't want to go far." He walked back to where Matt was standing. "I want to go the distance."

Matt shook his head. "You sure are a far cry from the confident guy I talked to two months ago. Ah, love—how it louses a person up." He laughed. Allowing himself a moment of camaraderie, he put his arm around Wayne's shoulder. "My advice, for what it's worth, is hang in there. If anyone can do it, you can. And Aimee's one hell of a girl."

Wayne's mood lightened. "Right, coach."

"Want Phyl to throw another little get-together?"

Wayne smiled in thanks but declined. "No, I'll go it on my own. Like you said, I got this far." He began to leave again.

Matt nodded, then called out, "What are your intentions?"

"To find Mulkowski, for openers," Wayne replied over his shoulder.

"I meant with Aimee."

Wayne knew he should have been annoyed at the question, but he knew Aimee drew out the protectiveness in people. Still, his feelings were new, raw, and he didn't want to share them until he was absolutely sure. "I'll let you know when I have it all sorted out myself."

Matt nodded. "Fair enough." He bit down on his cigar, then pulled it out again as Wayne walked back into the fire station. "And don't forget—"

"No Twinkies," Wayne finished for him.

Aimee changed tactics. She still made time for Wayne, still came by to help whenever she could—the house needed far more work than they'd anticipated—but she always brought Heather with her. She found it odd that she was using her own daughter as a chaperone, but Aimee needed her. Heather was there to protect her from herself as much as from Wayne.

If Wayne noticed Aimee's switch in behavior, he said nothing. Instead, he appeared to welcome Heather's company. Aimee would have been relieved, except that she suddenly realized that something else was happening. In bringing Heather along and keeping her between them, Aimee had turned them into a threesome. By trying to protect herself, she had inadvertently forged

them into a family unit without benefit of the proper
words or vows.

Every way she turned, Aimee thought in despair,
she was trapped—by Heather, by Wayne, by her own
actions and feelings.

And yet she continued to struggle.

Chapter 10

Aimee had always loved picnics, ever since she had first spread out a torn blanket in her backyard and served tiny sandwiches to her love-worn dolls.

Once a year Richard Boyce, the office manager, made a show of being human and hosted a picnic for all the agents and their families. Aimee always asked Emmett to join them, and it had become a tradition.

This year Heather wanted to stretch the tradition. She asked Aimee to invite Wayne. More accurately, she asked Aimee after the fact to sanction her inviting Wayne. Aimee's feelings for Wayne were growing more real, more tangible—and with them her fears—but she saw no way of countering Heather's invitation without leaving herself open to recriminations on all sides.

Giving in wasn't so bad, she decided.

They were in Heritage Park with all the other families. She sat on the edge of the blanket, her arms wrapped around her knees, watching Wayne and Heather toss a Frisbee back and forth.

"Makes a natural picture, doesn't it?" Emmett asked, nodding toward Wayne and Heather.

"Also a good Frisbee commercial," she answered noncommittally. Emmett hadn't let up since he'd seen Wayne play Monopoly with Heather; he seemed to have elected himself Wayne's unofficial campaign manager.

Pushing the Angels baseball cap back on his head, Emmett fixed Aimee with a stern look. "When are you going to wake up and smell the coffee?"

"I don't want coffee." She rested her head on her knees and averted her eyes. "I like tea. Nice, tranquil tea."

"Tea's got caffeine in it, same as coffee."

He was trying to snare her with rhetoric, Aimee mused. "Herbal tea," she clarified.

He clucked his tongue. "A person could miss a lot, drinking herbal tea."

Aimee was beginning to enjoy this. "I like an even keel. Slow and steady wins the race."

Emmett snorted. "Slow and steady finds that there's no reason to win the race. Everyone else has gotten up and gone home."

"Who's gone home?" Wayne asked as he collapsed onto the blanket.

Heather flopped down on her stomach. "Wow, am I ever tired!"

"That's a first." Aimee brushed back the curling damp hair from around Heather's forehead, then turned toward Wayne. "No one's gone home. Emmett was just quoting things he's read on embroidered tea cozies."

Wayne's eyes narrowed. "What's a tea cozy?"

"Something old-fashioned," Emmett replied. "Speaking of cozy…" He held out his hand to Heather, who immediately offered her shoulder to him for support. He pulled himself to his feet. "How about you and me getting ourselves some burnt hot dogs from the grill, little girl?"

"Sure." Heather was on her feet instantly. These days, Aimee thought, Heather always seemed to be hungry.

As the two left, Aimee glanced at Wayne. He had stretched out on the blanket—and looked totally comfortable. Aimee was very aware of his gaze on her. "A little obvious, wouldn't you say?" she remarked, inclining her head toward the departing duo.

Wayne smiled. The curl of his lips made her want to kiss him again. There was a sensuality to him that made her feel sexy, something she hadn't felt in a long time. She tried to block out the feeling.

"Maybe," he allowed. "But their hearts are in the right place." He twined a strand of her hair around his finger. "How about you, Aimee? Where's your heart?"

She wouldn't look at him. He seemed to be able to

read her so easily these days. "Same place it's always been."

"Under wraps," he said quietly.

Did he know how much he was tearing her apart? Until he'd come into her life, her resolution to keep her life untangled had been so easy to follow. Now her heart had been reawakened, like Sleeping Beauty, awakening to a kiss. His kiss. Why couldn't he have kept his damn lips to himself?

"Safe," she countered finally.

He skimmed his hand along her throat, then caressed her neck. The simple act brought all her emotions to the surface. She met his gaze.

"Do you really want to be safe, Aimee?"

She wanted to look away but couldn't. She wanted to say yes, but the lie wouldn't come. "No."

He tangled his fingers in her hair as he brought her head down to his level. After that the kiss seemed only natural.

Lightning sizzled through her veins. Her head was spinning even before his lips touched hers. Remotely she wondered what everyone else thought. She was kissing Wayne out in public, for all the world to see.

Her heart pounded, her brain hummed, as the kiss deepened and she fell headlong into it. She gave and gave and, in giving, took and started to become whole again.

They were both becoming whole. He wasn't sure exactly when it happened, when the idea had actually been born. Maybe it had come to him at that precise second. All he knew was that he wanted her in his life. Forever.

His mouth met hers in a dozen different ways, promising things he knew she was afraid to accept, promising things for both of them.

She broke away first, but it wasn't a break fueled by panic. Her eyes were still too misted over with desire for panic to have taken full control he knew.

She rested her hand on his chest and met his gaze. "That certainly wasn't safe."

"But nice," he murmured, playing with her hair, this time just to feel its silken texture. "Very, very nice."

He could tell that the smile that came to her lips was meant for him alone.

"Yes, it was."

The picnic, as it was every year, was a success. By evening everyone was tired but contented.

Wayne drove Aimee, Heather and Emmett home. Aimee thought she had never seen the old man move so quickly. He was out of the car and up the path to his house within seconds of the car's pulling up into the driveway.

Heather pulled a vanishing act as well as soon as Aimee unlocked the front door.

Wayne laughed as he took Aimee's hand in his. "I'm beginning to think we frighten them away."

"Don't you believe it. Emmett's probably peeking through his window right now, watching us. Heather, too."

As if to prove her right, Aimee saw the curtain at her front window move.

"Okay." Wayne wrapped his arms around her waist and pulled her toward him. She fit against him as if they had been created that way. "Let's give them something to watch," he urged.

Aimee thought the look in his eyes was just a little dangerous. "Wayne, I don't—"

"Yes, you do." He stopped her protests with his mouth.

She found it a wonderful, wondrous mouth, able to conjure up in her mind all sorts of kaleidoscopic images. He moved his lips away from her mouth, down to her jawline, then traced the planes of her neck.

Her breath came in shudders, and she curled her fingers into the palms of her hands as she tried to gain a semblance of control and keep her limbs from liquifying.

Each time he kissed her, Wayne found he wanted her more than the last time, even when the last time had been filled with incredible bittersweet longings. He wondered how long a man could go on wanting so much and not getting and still remain sane. He wasn't sure he had an answer to anything any longer, except to the question of his needs, which were all wrapped around Aimee.

When the kiss finally ended, he found it difficult to tell which of them was more shaken.

Aimee tried to make light of the situation. "Believe in giving people their money's worth, don't you?"

He leaned his forehead against hers. Their breaths mingled. "I certainly do try."

He made her happy, she marveled. Leading her to her own doom, he still made her happy. "You get an A for effort."

He touched her lower lip with the tip of his finger. "And for execution?"

"A plus."

"Well, at least the grades are good."

She grinned. "But you're *bad.*" She lengthened the last word into three syllables, the way Heather did whenever she was giving a compliment.

"If I were bad, Aimee Greer, you wouldn't be standing here on your porch getting kissed with the world looking on."

"Oh?" she asked innocently, trying to hide her excitement. "Where would I be?"

"In my three-quarters-finished house, in my new brass bed. In my arms."

His head still rested against hers, but the playfulness in his words was gone as he said, "I want to make love to you, Aimee. I don't know how much longer I can hold out."

Aimee straightened. He saw pain in her eyes. Whether it was there for him or for her, or for *them,* he wasn't sure.

His words had brought Aimee back to reality, brought her back to what she was allowing to happen. She couldn't take the risk in loving him. There wasn't just love to be faced, but the possible emptiness afterward. The deep, dark, all-consuming emptiness that had claimed her after she'd lost Terry. She had survived it once, but she was afraid she couldn't survive it again. "Wayne, we can't be more than friends."

He skimmed his hand down her hair. Slowly, he shook his head. "That wasn't a friend I just kissed."

"Yes, it was," she insisted.

"Aimee, we are friends. But also, we are—and will be—a lot more." She began to protest, but he put a finger to her lips. "I'll wait you out. And that is a promise."

She wrapped her arms around herself as she watched him walk back to his car. "Yes," she whispered softly, "I know it is." Suddenly she felt very cold.

Wayne let himself into his house twenty minutes later. He left the light off and made his way to the stairs, guided only by the moonlight that came in through the windows. The house was still in disarray, but in another few weeks he'd no longer have to share his home with workmen.

But would he ever share it with her?

He went to the window in his bedroom, the one Aimee had told him Louisa Maxwell had spent so many weeks looking through, waiting for her husband to return. The moonlight on the newly seeded lawn made it look almost silvery.

Silvery, like her hair. He could almost feel the silken texture against his fingers. Could almost feel her body curving into his.

Life was strange, he mused. When he'd left L.A., he'd been a man in search of something. When he'd found it, he hadn't been sure it was what he truly wanted. After all, there was something almost frightening about commitment. And she was a woman with a child, a ready-made family—and a ready-made ghost for him to be measured against.

Could he stand that? he thought suddenly. Could he stand wondering when he made love to her whether she was comparing the two of them?

He would make her put yesterday where it belonged, in the past. Today was theirs, and he was going to make her realize that. He felt it in every fiber of his body. She loved him; she just wasn't ready to admit it.

And as for the ready-made family, yes, it would take some getting used to, but wasn't a family what he'd wanted all along? Wasn't that what he'd ached for as a boy, sitting by himself, waiting for someone to come home, someone to talk to? He loved Aimee and he'd come to care about Heather. They could be a family. He had everything he'd ever wanted, right here before him. The only problem was to win it.

Wayne smiled as he walked away from the window. Winning had never been a problem for him.

"You know, if you don't marry that guy, I'm going to," Margo said abruptly after watching the delivery boy bring yet another rose to Aimee.

"You're already married," Aimee scoffed.

Margo shuffled over to her desk. "I won't tell him if you don't." She sighed, leaning over to smell the flower. "Any man who sends a woman a rose a day for over two months is a man worth making exceptions for." She straightened up as the front door opened. "Speak of the devil."

Aimee turned and saw Wayne coming toward her. Something bubbled inside of her. "Weren't you supposed to be working today?" she asked.

He dropped a quick kiss on her lips. "Hello to you, too."

She laughed. "I'm sorry. I only meant that you were off yesterday."

He counted his schedule off on his fingers for her again. "It's one day on, one day off, one day on, one day off, one day on, four days off. We're into the four-day stretch now."

She shook her head. "I can't seem to keep that straight."

He rested one broad, protective hand on her shoulder. "You will, after the wedding."

"Wedding?" Aimee echoed.

Margo's eyes were as big as saucers.

Wayne looked at the stunned woman. "Margo, can you take Aimee's calls for about an hour? She's going to lunch."

Margo came around. "You've got it, handsome."

Aimee put her hand on the papers on her desk. "But I have work to do."

He put an arm under hers and gently pulled her out of her seat. Aimee had a feeling that if she didn't go willingly, he'd carry her out. Possibly fireman-style. She opted to walk.

"And you'll do it a lot better after you build up your strength," he assured her.

Aimee barely had time to snatch her purse as Wayne hustled her out the door. "Are we eating or going to a gym?"

He opened the car door for her. "Whatever you want."

"Eating," she chose. "I hate exercise."

He looked her over. "For a woman who hates exercise, you certainly are in shape."

She couldn't miss the appreciative look in his eyes. She tried not to be pleased but knew she was. "Real estate people do a lot of walking up and down stairs," she quipped, sliding into his car.

He took her to a Japanese restaurant. As she followed the hostess to the back, where the private rooms were, Aimee had a nervous feeling that something out of the ordinary was about to happen. Once alone, she wavered between asking Wayne point-blank and keeping up a steady nonstop stream of words so that the conversation went only where she wanted it to go.

By the time they'd gotten through the sushi and the sake, she told herself that she was worrying needlessly. Her guard was completely down when the final course came. The hostess brought in a plate for Aimee. It was empty except for a blue box in the center.

"What is it?" she asked in a small, shaky voice.

"Why don't you open it and see?"

But she couldn't get her hands to pick the box up. All she could do was stare.

Unable to wait any longer, he took the box himself and opened it. A blue diamond gleamed against a velvet cushion.

Aimee licked her lips. "I thought only fortune cookies were supposed to have your future in them."

"I couldn't get a cookie that fit." He took the ring out of the box. "Put it on," he said coaxingly.

Her hands were frozen. Her heart felt as if it was going to explode in her chest. "I can't marry you, Wayne. I can't love you."

"It's not a wedding ring. It's an engagement ring."

"But engagements lead to weddings," she protested even as she ached to put the ring on.

"Maybe."

She looked up at him, startled. "Maybe?"

"Some people have been engaged for years. We'll keep the engagement going till you get used to the idea."

Because it was safer, she looked at the ring instead of at him. "It'd be a lie to wear this."

"Humor me. Let it grow on you. Let me grow on you." His voice was just short of seductive.

She couldn't keep staring at the ring. She looked up. It was her downfall. "That's the trouble. You already have. I'm afraid if I don't end it now I might do something stupid."

"Aimee Greer—" he kissed the corner of her mouth "—would never do anything stupid." He feathered his lips over to the other side of her mouth.

"Wayne," she protested.

He lifted her hand and slipped the ring on. "See? It doesn't even have to go on the left hand. It can start out on the right and move its way over."

She laughed sadly. "Rings don't move by themselves."

"No, people move them." He took her face between his hands and kissed her softly, deeply, and left her wanting more. "And when you're ready, you'll move the ring."

"Have you got that much patience, Wayne?" she asked, already loving him for it and damning herself at the same time.

"Surprisingly enough, yes. Patience is something a fireman learns to develop. You spend a lot of time waiting for the alarm to go off. But when it finally does, you spring into action a lot faster than the average person." He slid his finger down her nose. "And when *your* alarm finally goes off—and it will—I'll be ready to spring into action."

She leaned her head against his shoulder. He was being remarkably understanding for a man who had just been turned down. Was she a fool? Why couldn't she just let go? "You're one hell of a man, Wayne."

"That's what I've been trying to tell you all along."

She pushed back the tears that were suddenly clogging her throat. "Generous, too."

"I also walk little old ladies across the street whenever possible." He leered wickedly at her, then sobered. "But I'm no Boy Scout, Aimee."

She was glad they were in a restaurant. She knew that if they were home, alone, her resistance would have totally shattered. "I'll try to remember that."

"My gosh, you went and did it!" Margo exclaimed when she saw the ring on Aimee's finger. She was around her desk and at Aimee's side, grabbing her hand for a closer look. "But you've got it on the wrong hand."

"It's a friendship ring."

"And I'm going to lose ten pounds by sundown." Margo twisted Aimee's hand in the light. "This is the most gorgeous ring I've ever seen. The only rock bigger than this is in your head if you don't run off with that man posthaste."

Aimee sighed. "Margo, you don't understand."

"Maybe I don't," she conceded honestly. Her expression softened. "But I understand loneliness. Ten years from now Heather could be gone, married. Do you want to be by yourself?" She let Aimee's hand drop gently.

Memories came rushing back to Aimee, memories that now terrified her. "Terry and I made plans about growing old together, except that he never got a chance to carry them out. I'm not going to marry for security that might not come about."

"Then marry for a good time."

Aimee began pushing her papers into her briefcase. "This is a fascinating conversation, but I've got an appointment at two." She marched to the front door and shoved it open. As she walked out into the street, sunlight was reflected off her ring. Aimee looked down at it sadly, then let herself into her car. Her head ached. She wished there were a trick to clearing up confusion.

Chapter 11

It felt strange not to wear the ring. It had been there only a week, yet now that she'd taken it off, her hand felt oddly naked. She felt that way, too. Bereft. But she told herself it was the right thing to do. She'd given Wayne back his ring because she had to. Anything else would have been unfair to him. How could she tie him down to a woman who was so uncertain about her own feelings? A woman who might not ever be able to overcome her fears enough to be his the way he had a right to expect her to be?

When she was with him her thoughts, her doubts, tended to dim until all she saw was Wayne. But when she was away from him, her doubts would return with a vengeance. She never would have believed that she could actually love two men so much in one lifetime.

Yet she did. And loving brought with it the excruciatingly horrible fear of being left alone again.

She'd given the ring back to Wayne the night before. He'd come over to talk to her after she'd called him. She'd wanted to tell him over the phone but knew that was the coward's way out.

Wayne had known something was wrong when he'd heard her strained voice on the phone, but all the way over to her house, he'd told himself he was imagining things.

One look at her face told him he wasn't wrong. She was waiting for him on the front steps.

"What's the matter?" he asked as he got out of the car.

"Walk with me." She gave him her hand.

He took it without question, knowing that she'd tell him what was on her mind when she was ready. Her fingers felt tense. Suddenly he didn't want to know what she had to tell him.

There were stars out overhead. "Nice night for a walk," he commented. Aimee said nothing. "You know, Californians do entirely too little walking. They always seem to drive everywhere."

Aimee stared straight ahead. "Wayne, I have to return the ring you gave me."

"No, you don't." His voice was calm, almost detached. He struggled for control.

"Yes, I do."

Abruptly, she stopped walking and looked up at him.

He was angry, frustrated, confused. She looked pained to know that she was the cause of it.

"It isn't fair," she said quietly, slipping the ring from her finger.

He stared at her empty finger. "To whom?" His voice was steady but gruff.

She offered him the ring. He didn't take it.

"To you," she replied.

"Let me worry about what's fair for me." He pulled her against him. Air left her lungs in a little whoosh. "Damn it, you love me."

Aimee looked into his eyes. "Yes, I do."

"Well, then?" he demanded, impatient.

"Can't you see? That's the problem."

"No, I can't see it as a problem. People go their whole lives without finding someone to love them. You found it twice." He realized that he was holding her too tightly and let her go. "Why are you turning your back on something so precious?"

She looked away. "Because I don't want to be made to pay the same penalty again."

He gestured angrily, helplessly. "The death thing again." Wayne took hold of her shoulders and brought her line of vision back to him. He wasn't going to make it easy for her. "Is it because I'm a fireman?"

She shrugged beneath his grip. "Well, that certainly doesn't make it any easier."

Was he going to have to choose between her and his career? Frustration built within him. "Aimee, I can't quit. It's what I do best. It's what I need to do. Saving lives, making a difference, however small."

Her face was soft, appealing, as she tried to make him understand this one final time. "And I'm proud of you for that. I don't want you to quit."

His voice was hard, bitter. "You just want me to leave."

She sighed. "Yes."

He let her go and shoved his hands deep into his pockets to keep from shaking her until she came to her senses. "I don't understand you."

"Wayne, it's not because you're a fireman. I'd react the same way if you were an accountant." She pulled out his hand and pressed the ring into it.

He stared at the ring for a long moment, not believing the words that had been said, not believing that this was happening.

When he finally spoke, his voice was flat. "So what you're saying is that you're turning your back on what we have here because you're afraid."

Tears seeped through her lashes as she shut her eyes. "Yes," she answered hoarsely.

"Aimee…"

Opening her eyes, she reached up and touched his cheek tenderly. "I—Wayne, I'm sorry."

He pulled away, tired of tripping through mazes, tired of being patient, tired of being frustrated at every move. "Sorry doesn't even begin to cover it."

He closed his hand over the ring. There were a dozen

things he wanted to say to her. Perhaps half of them he would regret. Words of anger would settle nothing. They both needed some time to think, to sort out, to face the issue and decide if the path they had chosen was worth it.

"Tell Heather I said goodbye."

He turned and walked away from her.

After an entire sleepless night, Aimee didn't know what she realized anymore, except that her finger was empty and her life felt that way, too.

C'mon, she told herself. Three months ago, the man didn't exist for you and you managed. You were busy. You were happy.

She couldn't get herself to work, couldn't get herself to think of anything but Wayne. She'd never been so inert. She had escrow papers to file and a new house on the market to write up for the local newspaper. And she'd promised Heather that she would pick her up tonight right after the Fourth of July rehearsal.

The Fourth of July. Wayne was to have gone with them to the big celebration, and Heather had been so excited. She was involved in a fireworks display staged by the Y and she was anxious to do her best, to show Wayne how well she'd absorbed all the safety precautions he'd heaped on her.

Now he wouldn't be there.

It's what you wanted, isn't it?

No, she didn't know anymore what she wanted.

She looked up as the agency's front door slammed open, startling her. She half expected, half hoped that it was Wayne. But it wasn't; it was Emmett. He looked as upset as he had the day that his wife had died. Aimee rose in her seat.

"Emmett, what's the matter?"

He took her hands, and she suddenly realized that he was offering her comfort. "Emmett, what's wrong?" She didn't know why, but her heart began to pound.

"The Y's on fire. I just drove past it."

Aimee covered her mouth with both hands, a scream rising in her throat. "Oh, my God, Heather's in there!"

"C'mon." He took her arm. "I'll drive."

She ran ahead of him to his car.

"Did you see Heather?" she wanted to know. He said nothing as he guided the car down the next block. "Emmett, did you see Heather?"

"No." He forced the word out, then followed it up quickly with more. "But I was just driving down to the supermarket. There was a lot of smoke and commotion. I might have just missed her."

"Sure." Aimee clenched and unclenched her hands in her lap. "It's easy not to see one ten-year-old in the middle of things. She's bright. She'd get right out at the first sign of fire."

Heather had to be all right. She just had to be! She was just a child, with her whole life ahead of her.

Panic shredded away at Aimee's shaky courage.

When Emmett stopped the car, there were already

dozens of spectators held back by a fire line. Aimee jumped out of the car immediately and began pushing her way through the crowd. As she pushed, she searched.

"Heather!" she called, fighting to keep the panic from her voice. "Heather!"

But no one answered her desperate cry. As she fought her way to the front of the crowd, she saw a group of children. Heather's group. A sense of relief washed over Aimee until she realized that Heather wasn't in the group. She turned the child closest to her around to face her. The girl was bedraggled, with a smoke-streaked face, and she was obviously shaken.

"Dorothy." Aimee dropped down on one knee, still holding on to the child's shoulders. She tried to keep her voice from cracking. "Where's Heather?"

The blond braids bounced from side to side as Dorothy mutely told her that she didn't know.

Aimee released her and rose quickly. "Alice? Tracy?" She worked her way toward two other girls. "Have you seen Heather?"

"No, Mrs. Greer," the taller of the two girls answered.

Someone tapped her on the shoulder from behind. She swung around. It was another of Heather's friends.

"I think she's still in there, Mrs. Greer." The tall, red-headed girl with a smattering of freckles pointed toward the burning building. "She was going into the back room for the fireworks when Mrs. Brill saw the smoke."

A woman behind Aimee screamed as part of the building gave way to the flames.

He'd never get used to it. No matter how many fires he'd fought, no matter how many he would fight, he'd never get used to it. He felt his adrenaline pumping. Excitement and fear mingled within him. Fear for himself and fear for whoever might still be in the burning inferno. Each one was an inferno to him, an enemy to conquer. Wayne's fear spurred him on to do all he humanly could to save lives. It was what his life was all about.

"Damn these people! Why didn't they put in the sprinkling system the way you advised?" he shouted at Matt as they finished attaching the hose to the hydrant. He knew Matt had inspected the premises only a month ago.

"They said that the budget couldn't cover it this year."

"Is it going to cover this?" Wayne jerked his head at the burning building. And then he stopped and looked hard, stunned.

Matt turned around, and they both saw her at the same time. "It's Aimee!" Wayne yelled.

Aimee had ducked under the police barricade and was running toward the fire, her mind a blank except for one thought: She had to get to Heather. Nothing else mattered.

Strong hands came around her waist and literally lifted her in the air. She fought and kicked before she realized it was Wayne. "Let me go. Let me go," she begged. "Heather's still in there."

Wayne's expression froze as he set her down. Aimee wanted to collapse against him, but there was no time to seek comfort.

Matt was right behind him. "Mrs. Brill said everyone was out."

Aimee shook her head wildly. "She's not here. She's supposed to be here."

Wayne hurried back to the truck to get the equipment he needed. Aimee swung around to Matt. "Matt, please," Aimee cried, clutching at the sleeve of his rubberized coat, "you've got to let me go."

He looked around for someone to hold her back. "And have a dead woman on my hands? Aimee, the smoke'll get you before you get ten feet."

"I have to try!"

Wayne strode back. The visor on his helmet was up. In his hand he carried the mask for the self-contained breathing apparatus strapped to his back.

He gave Aimee a cold look that did more to calm her than all the comforting words in the world. "You have to stay put and wait!" He settled the mask over his face and pulled down the visor, then turned and walked into the building.

If it were possible to die twice, Aimee did as she watched him disappear. She stood, frozen in place, despite the jostling mob that crowded in around her. The noise in the background disappeared. She was alone, entirely alone, with nothing but her heart caught in her throat. Her whole world was in that building, she thought in agony. The two people she loved most could be dying right in front of her.

Tears flowed nonstop down her cheeks as she watched the hose's steady stream of water attack the flames.

An eternity went by. Where were they? Why was it taking so long?

She was a fool. She should have told Wayne before he went in that she loved him, should have told him that if he still wanted her, she'd marry him. Now he could be dead, and it was too late. If he were gone, she'd feel all the things she was afraid of feeling. It would be there, ring or no ring on her hand. Why hadn't she realized that? Why hadn't she taken the happiness when she had the chance?

She felt Emmett's hand on her shoulder. "They'll be fine, Aimee. Don't you lose hope."

She nodded, unable to speak. Placing her hand over his without looking away from the building, she clung to his words as if they were a promise. She desperately needed to cling to something.

Another part of the building crashed in flames, blocking the doorway. Matt and two other firemen hurried in to clear the debris away. The recreational building, all cedar wood, was old and brittle and burned like a tinderbox, despite the water.

Aimee bit down on her lower lip to keep from sobbing aloud. She was praying furiously when the door opened and Wayne staggered out, carrying an unconscious Heather.

A cheer rose from the crowd.

No one could have kept her behind the barricade this time. She ran toward them at lightning speed and reached Wayne, then was almost too terrified to ask. Heather looked so weak, so frail. So lifeless.

"Is she...is she...?"

"She's had a little too much smoke, but I think she'll be all right." His voice echoed within the mask.

Almost immediately, Aimee was being edged out of the way as two of the paramedics came over quickly with a gurney. Hands moving in well-practiced rhythm, they strapped Heather into it.

"You can ride with us to the hospital, ma'am," one of the attendants told Aimee.

As if anything could keep her away.

"Anyone else hurt?" the other attendant asked.

Matt shook his head. "There's no one else in the building, and she's the only one with any injuries." Relief etched in the premature lines on his face, he clamped his hand on Wayne's shoulder. "Terrific work, Montgomery. Really terrific work!"

Aimee turned just before she stepped into the ambulance. Wayne had taken off his helmet. His hair was soaked and clinging to his scalp. He looked drawn and harried.

"Thank you," she mouthed gratefully. The noise about them surged and swelled.

The ambulance driver closed the double doors behind her. She wasn't sure Wayne had gotten her message.

The attendant with them checked Heather's vital signs. "She's going to be just fine, Mrs. Greer."

"But she's still unconscious," Aimee protested, trying not to think of Wayne's drawn look. She took Heather's hand and held it tightly.

The attendant took his hand from Heather's wrist. "Yes, but her vital signs are all good." He smiled at Aimee. "She's a strong, healthy girl."

Aimee brushed back the bedraggled blond hair from Heather's forehead. "Yes," she whispered softly, more to herself than the attendant, "she is." Out the back window, she saw Emmett's car in the distance. He was following them. Aimee didn't let go of Heather's hand all the way to the hospital.

Chapter 12

By the time the ambulance arrived at the hospital, Heather had opened her eyes and given Aimee an entirely new lease on life.

Aimee hurried next to the cot, still holding Heather's hand, as the two attendants rushed the gurney through the doors.

Heather smiled weakly. "I guess I got saved."

Aimee held her tears back, knowing Heather never had understood crying when a person was happy. "I guess you did." How's that for understatement? she thought silently.

"How did I...?"

"Wayne."

Heather smiled, letting her eyes close. "I knew he would."

Aimee held Heather's hand all the way into the emergency-room examining area. Aimee was forced to wait outside in the hall, to pace and feel useless.

The prayers Aimee had uttered during the fire still ricocheted through her brain. But now they were prayers of thanksgiving. For Heather. And for Wayne.

Except for a twinge of anxiety, Aimee could see that Heather was going to be fine. As for Wayne, well, she didn't know about the "fine" part. She had done her very best to louse it up.

She was just going to have to be strong and right the wrong.

Could she repair the damage? Would he even want her to? Would he even want *her?* The look he had given her at the site of the fire was cold and stern and unlike anything she had ever seen on his face. It made her feel that they were strangers.

But cold look or not, she had died by inches waiting for him to return. She'd been afraid, as the flames did their best to eat away at the structure, that not only wouldn't Heather be coming back to her, but neither would he.

That was when the realization had hit her with full force. She loved him, and she might as well make the very most of it. Life didn't get better than this, and love was all that mattered.

She laced and unlaced her fingers, impatient to have her daughter back, impatient to see Wayne again. To talk to him and— And what? Ask his forgiveness. Yes, by God, if it came down to that. She wasn't so pigheaded that she'd let empty pride come between her and what was right.

And it was right. She saw it now, crystal clear.

Emmett shuffled over with a three-quarters-filled cup of lukewarm coffee. "Best damn hospital in the county, but they can't make coffee for beans." He pushed the cup into her hands.

Aimee smiled her thanks and drank, not tasting.

Emmett lowered himself down next to her on the bench. "She's going to be all right, Aimee."

Aimee nodded. "I know."

He frowned, his glasses slipping down his pointed nose. "Then why are you so down?"

"Do I look down?" she asked in surprise. Disheveled, yes, but down—no, that wasn't quite her mood. She drained the cup. "I was just thinking."

"About what?" He took the cup from her and tossed it into the wastepaper basket.

She couldn't help smiling. Privacy was a word Emmett had never become acquainted with. "About what you'll say when you finally get your wish."

The expression on his face was droll. "Cynthia and her husband are going to move out as soon as they ship him stateside?"

Aimee shook her head, knowing he was stretching this out. "Guess again."

He smiled. "You're finally going to give Wayne his due."

Aimee laughed, and the tension finally drained from

her. "I don't know about that, but I'll marry him if he'll still have me."

"Oh, he'll have you, all right. The wonder of it is that he didn't fling you over his shoulder and carry you off long before now."

"Emmett."

Emmett looked at her, becoming defensive of his opinion. "Well, the way he looked at you, like a boy in a candy store looking at an all-day sucker, a body couldn't see it any other way."

She tried to look serious and almost succeeded. "I don't think I quite care for the imagery."

He chuckled. "Guess you had to be there." He looked a little wistful. "They don't make all-day suckers anymore. Kids don't know what they're missing." He glanced down the hall and smiled. "Neither do you, but you will. Soon."

Aimee turned around and saw Wayne walking toward them. He was still wearing his fireman's uniform, although he'd changed out of his yellow rubberized suit. And, most important of all, he still wore that unapproachable look.

Emmett heaved himself to his feet. "Think I'll get some coffee myself."

Suddenly, she didn't want to be alone. She wanted Emmett to stay, as a buffer. To give her courage. "I thought you said it was awful."

"Always give everything a second chance, Aimee— that's my motto."

And then he was gone, leaving Aimee to feel suddenly very alone. And very much in need of Wayne.

He seemed to tower over her as he stood next to the bench. "How is she?"

Aimee took a long breath. "The doctor's with her now, but she came to just before they took her in." She smiled despite the fact that she felt utterly naked. "She said she knew you'd save her." Her smile faded as she grew more uncertain. "I don't know how to thank you."

Wayne wouldn't let himself be reeled in by that smile, by that aura of vulnerability about her. That had been his undoing before. He shrugged, looking around. "Just part of my job."

"Sit?" Aimee nodded toward the spot that Emmett had just vacated.

He looked at his watch uncertainly. "I've only got a few minutes." For the first time around her, he grew protective of his own feelings. "Matt wanted to know how you and Heather were, so I…"

She tilted her head toward him. "Volunteered to come and see for him?"

He sat down. "Something like that."

She wouldn't let the matter drop. If she was going to reopen channels between them, she had to prod. "Did you want to come on your own?"

Why was she doing this? he wondered. What was she trying to get at? That he still wanted her? Why? What would that prove? He paused for a moment. When he spoke, his voice was tight.

"Aimee I think we've been this route before, and like you've told me, it doesn't lead anywhere."

He stared down at his hands. They were folded, tense. This time, it wasn't just the normal winding down of adrenaline that he always felt after fighting a fire. This time the tension had to do with her.

"I don't always know what I'm talking about," she said.

He directed his gaze at her. Was that her way of saying…?

No, he wasn't going to open that door again unless he was damned sure it wasn't going to be slammed in his face.

"The Y's a complete loss," he said almost carelessly.

"Oh."

He heard the pain and concern in her voice. It was one of the things he loved about her. But right now, it angered him. She was always so concerned with things, but when it came to him— He let the anger go. It served no purpose. She was what she was.

"I suppose you'll be heading up a committee to raise funds to have it rebuilt."

He sounded disinterested, as if he were making polite conversation. He hadn't sounded this distant even when they'd first met. Aimee felt a stab of pain but refused to give up. "Why would you suppose that?"

"Well, aren't you always heading up some committee or other?"

"Maybe, in the past, before I had more important

things to do." Why was this so hard? Had she come to her senses too late? No, she wasn't going to let it be.

"What kind of more important things?"

"Being your wife," she said awkwardly, then raised her eyes to his. "If you still want me."

He wanted to take her into his arms and vanquish her hesitant question with his mouth against hers. But he had been burned once, and he wanted to be sure she wasn't going to swing back to the other end of the spectrum again. "What made you change your mind?" he asked quietly.

"Today I nearly lost everything. It made me stop and see things clearly. When you went in after Heather, I realized that I could be losing you without ever having had you." As she spoke, she took hold of his arm. He didn't respond. But he didn't take it away, either. Hope began to blossom. "I know that there are no guarantees in life, but I also realize that I'd be a fool not to accept happiness when it's right here in front of me."

He nodded thoughtfully. "Yes, you would be."

She lifted her brows. "You could at least have the decency to tell me I'm not a fool."

For the first time since she'd seen him today, he grinned.

"You're not a fool. Otherwise, you'd still be saying no."

She had to ask, had to hear him say it. "Then you do still want me?"

"Only if you'll stop being an idiot and not ask such

stupid questions. I've wanted you since I first saw you."
He fumbled in his shirt pocket, then smiled, relieved,
as he drew something out. "Here."

Aimee stared down at the ring in the palm of his
hand. "You have it with you?"

His shoulders lifted slightly. "I didn't have any place
to put it, and I thought maybe if I carried it around I'd
find a use for it."

"Wait." She stopped him as he moved to put it back
on her finger.

"Changed your mind again?"

She didn't answer. Instead, she twisted off her
wedding ring, then put out her hand. Her left hand.

"No, and I'm not about to. Ever again."

She felt his hands tremble a little this time as he
slipped the ring on. Aimee felt a tug at her heart. She
ran her newly decorated hand through his hair. "I really
do love you, you know. I realized that married or not, I
love you, and if anything happened to you I would suffer
just the same, so I might as well get a little of the benefits
of loving you as well as suffering the consequences."

He laughed. "Not exactly romantically put, but I can
accept that."

"You'd better. I've accepted the fact that a woman
can love just as deeply twice in her lifetime, and if
she's lucky enough to get the chance, she should snatch
it up and run like hell."

"No." He touched her lip with the tip of his finger,
outlining it. "Not run. You're never running again."

"No," she agreed just as he lowered his mouth to hers, "I'm not."

A polite cough separated their lips but not their arms. Aimee looked up to see a man in a long white lab coat who was eyeing them with a bit of amusement.

"I take it you two already know the news, then?"

Aimee jumped to her feet. "Oh." She suddenly came to. "About Heather."

"Yes, I'm very happy to say that she's just fine. Nothing a day in bed isn't going to cure."

"May I take her home now?" Aimee asked.

"I think you'd better." The doctor smiled down at Aimee. "She's getting very restless. Says she has to thank someone named Wayne for saving her life. The way she's talking, I think she has him confused with Superman."

Aimee looked at Wayne. When had she ever felt this wonderful?

"Not confused. Correctly labeled." She turned toward the doctor and took his hand. "Thank you."

"I had nothing to do with it. That person named Wayne deserves all the credit." Someone called to him and the doctor nodded his goodbye.

Aimee smiled as Wayne slipped his arm around her. "And he's going to get it, too," she warned him.

"Sounds ominous," Wayne said, whispering in her ear.

"Mister," she began with a mischievous twinkle, quoting a line he had once said to her, "'you ain't seen nothin' yet.'" She nodded toward Heather's room. "C'mon, let's go tell Heather that her matchmaking days are over and that Superman's about to become her daddy."

"Am I going to have to leap tall buildings?"

"Only for me." She reached up and took his lapel. "Privately." Her breath tingled the planes of his face.

He winked. "You've got it."

"Yes, I really have. I just didn't know it before."

Wayne and Aimee went into Heather's room together.

* * * * *

Fall in Love with...

MEN
in UNIFORM

YES! Please send me the exciting *Men in Uniform* collection. This collection will begin with 3 FREE BOOKS and 2 FREE GIFTS in my very first shipment—and more valuable free gifts will follow! My books will arrive in 8 monthly shipments until I have the entire 51-book *Men in Uniform* collection. I will receive 2 free books in each shipment and I will pay just $4.49 U.S./$5.39 CDN for each of the other 4 books in each shipment, plus $2.99 for shipping and handling.* If I decide to keep the entire collection, I'll only have paid for 32 books because 19 books are free. I understand that accepting the 3 free books and gifts places me under no obligation to buy anything. I can always return a shipment and cancel at any time. My free books and gifts are mine to keep no matter what I decide.

263 HDK 2653   463 HDK 2653

Name	(PLEASE PRINT)
Address	Apt. #
City	State/Prov.	Zip/Postal Code

Signature (if under 18, a parent or guardian must sign)

Mail to the **Harlequin Reader Service:**
IN U.S.A.: P.O. Box 1867, Buffalo, NY 14240-1867
IN CANADA: P.O. Box 609, Fort Erie, Ontario L2A 5X3

* Terms and prices subject to change without notice. Prices do not include applicable taxes. Sales tax applicable in N.Y. Canadian residents will be charged applicable taxes. This offer is limited to one order per household. All orders subject to approval. Credit or debit balances in a customer's account(s) may be offset by any other outstanding balance owed by or to the customer. Please allow 4–6 weeks for delivery. Offer available while quantities last. Offer not available to Quebec residents.

Your privacy: Harlequin is committed to protecting your privacy. Our Privacy Policy is available online at www.eHarlequin.com or upon request from the Reader Service. From time to time we may make our lists of customers available to reputable third parties who have a product or service of interest to you. If you would prefer we not share your name and address, please check here. ☐

MUBPA10

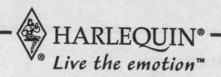

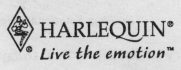

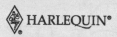

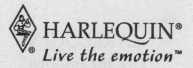

HARLEQUIN®
INTRIGUE®

BREATHTAKING ROMANTIC SUSPENSE

Shared dangers and passions lead to electrifying romance and heart-stopping suspense!

Every month, you'll meet six new heroes who are guaranteed to make your spine tingle and your pulse pound. With them you'll enter into the exciting world of Harlequin Intrigue— where your life is on the line and so is your heart!

THAT'S INTRIGUE—
ROMANTIC SUSPENSE
AT ITS BEST!

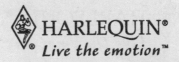

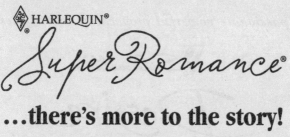

HARLEQUIN®

Super Romance®

...there's more to the story!

Superromance.
A *big* satisfying read about unforgettable
characters. Each month we offer *six* very different
stories that range from family drama to adventure
and mystery, from highly emotional stories to
romantic comedies—and much more! Stories
about people you'll believe in and care about.
Stories too compelling to put down....

Our authors are among today's *best* romance
writers. You'll find familiar names and talented
newcomers. Many of them are award winners—
and you'll see why!

If you want the biggest and best
in romance fiction, you'll get it
from Superromance!

Exciting, Emotional, Unexpected...

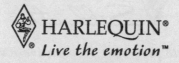

HARLEQUIN®
Live the emotion™

passionate powerful provocative love stories

**Silhouette Desire® delivers
strong heroes, spirited heroines
and compelling love stories.**

Silhouette Desire features
your favorite authors, including

Ann Major,
Diana Palmer,
Maureen Child
and Brenda Jackson.

**Passionate, powerful and provocative
romances *guaranteed!***

For superlative authors, sensual stories
and sexy heroes, choose Silhouette Desire.

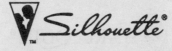

passionate powerful provocative love stories